Narcissistic Episode

Series

Amy Perry
MS
Psycology

Amy Perez MS

Psychology

Published 2019

Copyright 2019

ISBN: 978-1674802329

Printed by Amazon

Front Cover Design by Author.

Book Design by Designer.

Author: Amy Perez MS Psychology

https://www.amazon.com/kindle-dbs/author/ref=dbs_P_W_auth?_encoding=UTF8&author=Amy%20Perez%20MS%20Psychology&searchAlias=digital-text&asin=B07H24NKYJ

Episode 1

1

"Baby! We have new neighbors! And they have kids!" He sure is handsome. My husband. I cannot believe we're married. What a dream come true.

"That's great sweetheart. Oliver will have someone to play with." Mitch grabs the chicken to put it on the grill. This is fancy compared to our usual hot dogs and hamburgers. I swear, I thought we were done being broke. Until Mitch took an internship.

"Baby can you grab the melted butter off of the counter?"

"Sure sweetie." I walk through the sliding glass door. Things will get better, they always do. I peak into the living room to see a zombie.

At least that's what I call Oliver when he's engrossed in video games. He is staring the screen with his bright blue eyes. I glance at his blonde hair. It's getting kind of long. I guess I can charge a haircut on my credit card. Oh yeah, butter.

This is a special night. It's Friday. Typically, Mitch would be working nights and weekends in the service industry. But not anymore. He's an intern and he works normal hours. Thank God. This is all I've ever wanted. Oliver and I have spent so many nights, weekends and holidays alone. I walk through the door to see Mitch talking to a man. He is the definition of Caucasian.

He has light skin, blue eyes and dirty blonde hair. He is skinny but muscular. It is a vast difference against Mitch's dark features.

Being Italian gives him an authentic look. The men look pretty infused in their conversation. I quietly walk up with the butter and set it on the grill.

2

Ah, the kickoff of spring. This winter was rough and freezing. That's how New York is though. But the city is gorgeous. You just have to take the good with the bad. My family is minutes away. The school systems are great. My husband and I are in great schools. Back to work for me.

I walk into the kitchen and adjust my mannequin. She is wearing a fashionable red top. I should make about fifteen dollars off of it. It isn't what I planned on doing for work. But I can't afford child care in the area. Plus, it keeps me busy. Not that I need it. Studying psychology is pretty tough. My neuropsychology class is kicking my ass.

I snap a few photographs of my mannequin. Hey money is money. It's not forever. Honestly, it's pretty enjoyable. I glare out of the door wall of our townhouse to see the men laughing. Looks like we will get along with our new neighbors. The smell coming in from the grill is intoxicating.

"Baby, come here for a sec." Mitch waves a hand.

3

I pull open the screen door. The screen is hanging off of the frame. The life of having a dog and a cat. I manage to crack a smile. What is it called smiling depression? A great way to hide the pain. I am really good at it. Mitch is able to see right through it though. I do enjoy that he can light a match in my darkness.

"Hi, how are you?" I give a nice smile. "My name is Noelle."

"Chance. Chance Robins."

"Nice to meet you Chance."

His eyes are crystal blue. They seem to pierce right through me.

"You are going to love this area. The school system is great for your children."

"Oh no, they aren't mine."

I stare at him blankly. I don't want to judge or make any cliché reactions. I don't exactly come from the most picture-perfect background myself.

4

"Can I grab you a beer Chance?"

"Sure, that'll be great."

I turn to walk away. That guy doesn't seem super respectful. His demeanor. He definitely feels superior, that is obvious. I grab a Bud Light out of the fridge.

This is the shittiest beer ever. At least for me. It's safe though. Everyone loves it. Should I shake it up? Knock him down a peg? I pulled the prank on my Grandfather when I was about seven. He wasn't too happy. Thank goodness he had a good sense of humor though. I'll play nice, for now. I gently twist the cap off and toss it on the counter.

"Oliver, dinner is almost ready," I call out to my little angel.

"Okay Daddy!" I check the boiling corn on the stove. It isn't quite time for sweet corn yet but it will be pretty good. I poke each corn on the cobb with a fork to get them to spin. Just about done.

I hear Mitch bust out laughing. I just want him to be happy. He deserves the world. Life isn't exactly easy at the moment. However, we are healthy and the weather is finally warm.

5

Personally, I love the snow. I love to play in it with Oliver. I love sipping coffee while watching the snow fall outside my window.

"Here baby."

Mitch reaches out a hand for the cold beer. I'll let Mitch handle Chance. I haven't made my mind up on him yet. Two blonde haired girls come running behind the row of townhouses. Their blonde curls are blowing in the breeze. How cute, I can see a resemblance.

So, what did Chance mean by the fact that they weren't his? Was he kidding? Are they adopted? Mitch and I adopted Oliver when he was a baby. We were so happy. The day that we got approved to be foster parents was the best day of our lives.

6

I don't want to be the nosey neighbor type though. That's not my style. Eventually, I will hear their story. I am really good at getting people to open up. It happens everywhere I go. People just end up telling me their whole life story.

I guess that's why I am in school to become a psychologist. I love to hear people's life story. Plus, I have a family history of mental illness. It just makes sense.

I turn the burner off and cover the corn. It just needs to sit for ten minutes and it'll be done. Mitch and Chance seem to be getting along great. Stop it Noelle. Don't be so jealous all of the time. I hate that about me.

7

That is my least favorite personality trait. I try so hard to hide it. I am always jealous of my sister too. It isn't because she is a woman. It's just that I feel like her and my Mom are closer than I am to them. I know it's dumb. I just can't stop it. It's just like I don't have the same connection. I do like some of the same things as they do. I just don't have enough time for shopping and going out like I used to. Oliver takes up all of my time.

I just love him, I really do. I just never feel like I am enough. I definitely took on the Mommy role right away. Hopefully he isn't confused by having two Dads. Hell, sometimes I'm confused. What should Mitch and I each be responsible for?

I even get jealous if him and Oliver are closer than Oliver and I. Ugh, as much as I want to be a psychologist, I feel like I am the one who needs the help. I plop down on the couch next to Oliver and place my hand on his knee.

"Hey Buddy."

Oliver gives me a glance. Then he stares back at the screen. My little zombie. Good thing he only gets an hour a day.

All of the sudden I hear shattering glass. What the hell? I jump up from the couch to check on Mitch. My fight or flight mode has been activated.

Episode 2

1

"Babe, he tripped!" Mitch yells from outside.

Chance stands up with a confident smile. Beer is covering his sliding glass door. I run over and grab a paper towel roll. A woman with blonde hair, tattoos and piercings comes around to the backyard. She is fairly straight-faced. She should seem more excited for just moving into a new place. I run over and reach the paper towel over the fence.

"Thanks man, I appreciate it."

"You're bleeding."

Chance looks down at his hand. He doesn't look phased. That's weird.

"Shit." Chance whips open his door and stomps inside.

Mitch grabs the chicken of off the grill as if nothing even happened. How can he be like that? He has such a lack of empathy. Especially for strangers. He seems to only genuinely care for Oliver and I.

He always seems very obsessed with me. He is overly involved in my life. If we get into an argument, he won't even let me walk away. He follows me. Honestly, he scares me sometimes.

He was ordered to take anger management classes when he was a teenager. If it wasn't for my Father, I would probably question him more. My Father loves him. He is always bragging about Mitch. He says that he gained another son the day we got married.

2

"Baby, you going to help me out?" Mitch is slicing the chicken on a cutting board.

"Yes boss."

Mitch doesn't say anything. He typically doesn't reply to my sarcasm. I feel like one day, he is just going to snap.

I grab a pair of tongs and grab his butt with them. He gives me a side eye. I know he is stressed about the new job. I get it. I'm just trying to break the tension.

"Can you clean up those clothes and your mess?"

Damn. Okay. I wanted to work after dinner but Mr. Clean freak has other plans. He gets it from his Mother. I am a clean person, but damn. They want perfection. It is literally impossible to keep a house perfect. Especially with a young child. He is always experimenting and making messes.

I grab Sally to take her down to the basement. That's the name of my mannequin. My sister taught me to sell clothing online. I named my mannequin after the store that we buy clothing from to resell.

This basement gives me the creeps. It is cold and unfinished. All of the brick townhouses in our row have the same creepy basement. If one floods, then they all flood, it's the worst. I set Sally in the corner. I glance over at Mitch's technology bins. They are off limits to Oliver and I. Mitch is a huge video gamer. He goes live on the computer three times a week. He has gained thousands of followers this year. I am happy for him. And of course. Jealous.

"Babe!"

"Coming!"

I walk up the wooden basement stairs to darkness. What the heck? There are two candles lit on the table. Mitch is standing at the table with roses. I give him a surprised smile.

"They were in my car." Mitch hands me a card. He really is so sweet. I peel open the envelope. It's a thank you card. I start to read the inside. A tear falls from my cheek

3

How does he always do that? He always makes me cry. He is so sentimental.

"I love you." Mitch leans in for a kiss.

Our passion hasn't dwindled in our fifteen years together. We have been through so much and hard times. The worst was when I got diagnosed with manic depression. Even though it was devastating, it was a relief. We finally had an explanation for my behavior.

We found out why I would explode with anger and irritability. It explained my sleepless nights. No matter how bad it got, Mitch stayed by my side. Literally, everyone in my life has either shied away or walked away. Except for Mitch.

We embrace each other in a long hug. Just what I needed.

"Baby, it's Chance."

Mitch backs away. "You're jealous of him?"

"No, it's Chance, he is staring in our window."

Mitch turns to look outside. Chance is standing by his fence glaring in our window.

"Maybe he likes red heads with green eyes." Mitch pokes me in the arm.

"So, not funny!"

"Fuck him, he's a weirdo babe."

How is Mitch like that? Literally, nothing phases him. I am officially creeped out. Does he have a problem with gay people? It wouldn't be the first time we have encountered it.

Oliver comes running into the kitchen.

"Yummy!" He shouts.

Mitch and I bust out laughing. Oliver is so dang cute. He keeps us on our toes, that's for sure.

4

Mitch pulls out a bottle of Meiomi Pinot Noir. It's the wine we bought the night we got engaged. Wow, he is pulling out all of the stops. Shit. He must have to go out of town. Dammit. His new job. He mentioned them having him go to Mexico. It's the worst. But the positive side is that he will bring in more money.

"So, when do you leave?"

Mitch let's out a sigh. "In the morning."

"It's okay, Oliver and I can hang out with my Dad."

"Okay my baby."

Mitch twists open the cap to the wine. The wine glasses are already on the table. Oliver is already digging into his chicken. Mitch put some melted butter in a dish on the side of his plate.

Oliver sure is fancy. I don't exactly want to be left alone with the new neighbor.

5

He gives me the creeps. He seems like the guy that all of the girls drool over but deep down he is really a douche bag. Mitch pours our wine as I take my seat. I am just feeling so grateful for where we are in life. Life really is good.

"Oliver, sweetie, do you want some salt on your corn?"

"Yes please."

"Baby, I'm going live tonight."

"Of course, you are, got to give the followers some action." I give Mitch a playful wink and smile.

6

Ah, so perfect. I am loving this basement. At first, I thought I could use it to practice karate. But now I know of something better. For now, it will be the new home for my pieces. My puzzle pieces that is. I have built quite the collection. The taste of Jack Daniels and Coke crosses my lips. The sweet taste rolls off of my tongue. I am building the most beautiful sculpture. The female body.

It is going to be a masterpiece. It just takes time. My way of getting the pieces isn't exactly easy. The last one was the fight of my life. I turn on my computer to get started. My research.

Each candidate must be carefully planned out. The skin color must be perfect. These damn camera filters that the girls are using is making it difficult.

I don't mind the challenge though. I have already planned my next piece of my puzzle.

"Hello Jolene." A smile crosses my face. Why is this so exciting? Puzzles are just so exhilarating. Once you find the right piece, you can feel so relieved. The stress just melts away. I hear tiny footsteps upstairs. I better make this quick.

Episode 3

1

"Hello, hello peeps! What's happenin'?"

I can hear Mitch being quite the entertainer. We finally found good use for the basement. Besides storing all of my clothes for the store.

"Come on Oliver, let's get you in the bath."

Oliver and I head up the stairs to our bathroom. This isn't the best place to live but it isn't the worst. It has a backyard but it's very small. I've always wanted a big backyard for Oliver to play in. Him and I could kick a ball and chase each other.

Not to mention our dog Boots. He is a beagle boxer. He resembles a boxer more. He has really outgrown this townhouse. I just feel like I failed somehow.

I turn the water to warm in the tub for Oliver.

"Come on buddy, get your clothes off and hop in."

"Will you get in with me Daddy?"

I'm not sure if he is getting too old to take baths with me. I wear my swimming trunks but still, he is getting older.

Oliver started pre-kinder this year. He just turned five in the winter.

"Come on Daddy!"

2

"Okay buddy, hang on." I walk into mine and Mitch's bedroom. Our view isn't too great.

It's of the parking lot and the dumpsters. It is convenient for throwing out trash though. However, Mitch and I long for a condo on the water. It just seems so selfish. I want to give Oliver the best life.

I see a silhouette of a person by the dumpster. Male. Medium build. He is throwing out small tied grocery bags. That's weird. He has like fifteen bags. The man is looking back and forth by the street before he throws out each bag.

The person turns in my direction. Shit. It's Chance. My curtains are wide open. His eyes glare into my window. Don't mind me as I stand here in my underwear staring at you.

3

This isn't exactly the best first impression. I rip my curtains closed. It's his fault. He shouldn't be acting shady by a dumpster.

"Daddy, come on!"

I quickly change into my swimming trunks. I remove my Apple watch and set it on my night stand. Mitch would have a fit if I get it wet. As if I care about that stuff. I would rather have a leather engraved bracelet. Or maybe a seashell necklace.

"Hey buddy." Oliver is waiting patiently by the tub. He has about twenty toys ready for our bath. Mitch doesn't like it. I think it's great germ control.

Oliver and I throw all of the toys in.

"Are we gonna play basketball Daddy?"

"Of course, buddy."

Our version of basketball is when I throw the toys at him and he has to catch them. Each toy is assigned points in advance. The points range from one to infinity.

"Catch buddy."

"Oh no, I missed."

"That's okay! Try again!"

All of the sudden the door swings open. It's Chance. What the hell?

4

"Hey honey, it's just us," Mitch chimes in. Chance is holding a white electronic in his hand.

"Chance has a carbon monoxide detector for us."

"Oh okay, that's great." Even though it's awkward timing. "You never can be too safe," I chime in. "Ow!" Oliver threw a Lego at my face. "No Oliver!"

"Ten points!" Oliver laughs.

Mitch looks over angrily.

"It's okay," I lie.

I will talk to him about it later. I will save the whole teachable moment for next time. Perhaps when I am not half naked in front of our new neighbor.

Chance removes the hair dryer from the plug and puts in his device. It has a blinking green light.

Mitch and Chance walk out of the bathroom and close the door.

"Oliver, you don't throw stuff at people's faces when they aren't looking. That's not nice."

Oliver looks down into the water looking ashamed.

"Okay?"

"Okay Daddy."

I feel like I spoil him too much because he is an only child. I give into everything. I wonder if I am being too soft. I never even thought I would have a child of my own. Growing up when I was a child, it was unheard of to be gay.

Now, it seems perfectly normal. Thank goodness. Mitch is such a macho man that people never believe him. Until they see me. I am not sure if it's my long red hair or the fact that I am always wearing something pink. Pink is my favorite color.

It wasn't always my favorite. When I was a boy, I loved the color blue, playing sports and playing outside. But one day, I just changed and became a more beautiful version of myself.

"Alright Oliver, let's get out and dry off."

"No, no, five more minutes."

"Okay, but I'm getting out."

Oliver engrosses himself in private play with his toys. I love when kids get lost in pretend play. There is just something innocent about it.

5

Back down to my basement. I have planning to do. Plus, my Jack and Coke isn't going to finish itself. Noelle is quite the Dad. Taking a bath with his son like that. It's cute actually. I wish I could be more like that. More carefree. But I'm not. I'm cold. I only put on a show. My loved and friends see a calm and collected guy. A masculine demeanor. Don't forget my fake smile. Never forget the fake smile. Anything can be hidden behind a smile. Pain, lies, murder.

I click the tab on my computer. Some people shop on Amazon. But me? I prefer Instagram. The women are so beautiful. Surrounded by flowers or lying on the beach. I am always tempted to private message them but I never do. That's how I manage to never get caught. Not a like, comment or follow. However, tempting it might be. I just scroll on through minding my business.

My puzzle piece business that is. It has nothing to do with them. It's all about me in the end. It's my wants and my needs.

6

Living in New York makes things complicated. There are always people everywhere. Thank goodness for traveling. I deliver myself. Hey, I'm a nice guy like that. But my next girl, she's a local. I am taking a huge risk I know. But there is something about her skin. It's so white and porcelain-like.

Her makeup is done just so. It must take her at least an hour. She cares about her appearance. And I care about mine. I choose very carefully. And her teeth, they are perfect. She looks like a famous person. She sort of is famous. She has over three thousand followers. What does that even mean anyway? Will they even notice when she doesn't share a picture of her meal or drinks with friends?

7

I should feel bad for this but I don't. It's been five years since my last kill. I have been so good. My palms are starting to sweat. Social media has come a long way since last time. I used to have to do this old school. I have been practicing stalking down women for two years now. Let's call those women my beta testers. Thank you, ladies. I have it down to a science now. I'm confident. I'm good.

I take a sip of my sweet drink. The ice has watered it down a bit. Just how I like it. I slam the rest of my drink. The alcohol fills my stomach. I grab a cigar out of my pack. It's time to head outside for a smoke. I put in my work.

I close the tab on my computer. Just a little innocent scrolling. No big deal. Goodbye for now Jolene. You will be at karaoke this Sunday and so will I. I will clap extra loud when you sing Gwen Stefani songs. I might even buy you a vodka tonic.

I turn the computer off and head up the wooden steps. What can I say? Life is good. I have it all. I really am a great guy. I walk out onto my back porch and light up my cigar. Someone is sitting in the dark, crying. It's Noelle. Fake smile time.

Episode 4

1

"I was diagnosed as being narcissistic four years ago. My wife left me a year later. It's not my fault."

I put a hand on Chance's shoulder. Should I open up about me? My family? I really wasn't expecting a heart to heart this soon with Chance. I guess anything can happen when you are smoking a blunt in the backyard. Our old neighbors were cool with it.

"It's okay Chance. I have a lot of experience with mental illness." I set the weed filled blunt into my ash tray. I'm not too good at rolling them. Usually Mitch does it but he's been so busy with his fans.

"Well you are the big shot psychologist, it makes sense."

I let out a laugh. "Student, Chance. Key word there."

"Student Shmudent," Chance says and busts out laughing.

I can't hold back my laughter. That was a good one. Our hysterical laughter fills the night sky.

2

I hear some ruffling in the bushes. Chance and I give each other a terrified stare. What the hell? One time when I was out here smoking, an animal brushed up against my leg. It scared the shit out of me.

"Hello?" I hear a familiar voice.

"Dad?"

"Noelle?"

"Dad? What are you doing?" It's late and his house is an hour away.

"I gotta talk son."

Chance stands up slowly. He gives my Father a respectful nod. He walks over to his yard.

"Take it easy Noelle."

"Dad, are you okay?"

My Father plops down into a chair. He lets out a sigh.

"It's Cherry."

My mind goes to panic mode. "Is she okay?"

"Yeah son, she's fine."

I breathe a sigh of relief. Even though she is my Dad's girlfriend, she is like my second Mom.

"I'm leaving her."

I wait patiently for an explanation. My Dad gave her fifteen years. I knew they had their struggles but this comes as a surprise. I would offer him a hit off my blunt but he is more a cigarette kind of guy. He would benefit from it. He needs to relax a little.

"You okay?"

He doesn't say anything.

3

He just stares off into the distance. He has done that ever since I was a child. It's like he gets lost in thought.

"You want a pop Dad?"

"Sure son, that'll be great."

I get up to leave him with his thoughts. I make sure to keep cold ones in the fridge for him. Pepsi that is. He isn't a drinker. I don't blame him. His whole life, he has dealt with alcoholism in his family.

He would never drink even if everyone around him did. Someone once bashed him at a party for wasting a beer. Thankfully my Grandma stuck up for him. She doesn't take shit from anyone. I should be more like her.

"Hi Boots." My dog loves the sound of me grabbing for ice. If I drop a piece of ice, he hits the jack pot. He will grab the ice cube and scurry into the living room. Why can't people be as easy as dogs? Dogs love you no matter what. On my worst day, Boots is always by my side. I reach down and hand Bootsie a piece of ice. As usual, he takes off running with it. Cigarette smoke fills up my kitchen. Shit.

4

Mitch is going to be pissed. I run over and slam the door wall shut. Both of my parents smoke cigarettes and Mitch hates it. It makes him super mad if smoke comes into the house. I can't blame him though. He lost a friend in high school to cancer. Both of his parents smoked in the home. His friend died from lung cancer.

I fill a glass with ice and pour some pop in. Just the way Dad likes it. It's the little things with him. He is always so appreciative. I bring over the glass and pull the door closed behind me. I make sure to slam it shut. I definitely don't want to hear Mitch complaining.

My Dad is slumped down with his elbows on his knees. He just looks defeated. He looks beat up by life. As much as I idolize him, I don't want to end up like him. I thought him and Cherry would be together forever. I set the glass next to my Father and sit next to him.

He may open up or he may not. He's unique that way. Sometimes he is ready to talk about feelings. I try to be open with him. But I can't always be one hundred percent. It's like I'm still that shy little boy who is scared to be scolded.

5

My Dad only spanked me once. But that was enough. I am terrified to make him mad. I guess that makes me sort of a people pleaser. I try my best to make everyone happy. I pull the rubber band from my long red hair and let it fall to my shoulders. I breath in the sweet spring air. There is a dampness that makes it feel cold.

My Dad shoots me a look. He hates my long hair. "You look like your mother."

I look down, I don't want to hear the lecture.

"You look good son."

I look at him surprised. Approval. That's all I ever want from him. I don't know why. I should be an independent adult. I shouldn't be so worried about what people think all of the time. A cloud of cigarette smoke hits my face. I don't react. I don't care. I'm desperate. I'm not crazy about cigarette smoke but I'll do anything to be close to my Dad. His time and attention mean everything to me.

A lot of people seem to use him for his money but not me. I don't want a dime from him. I wasn't always like that though. I used to use him too.

When I was a teenager, I would purposefully wear old, tights clothes when it was his time for visitation. He would take one look at me and take me to the mall. Why was I so manipulative like that? I took advantage of him.

Did he know what I was doing? I took advantage of him just like everyone else. Doesn't he see through it? Does he enjoy getting used? It's like everyone sees it but him. Anytime people ask him for money, he says yes. If someone wants something in his house, he gives it to them. It's like he doesn't know how to say no.

"Dad, you can stay with me while you figure things out."

"I don't wanna put you out son."

"Dad, I insist."

6

My Dad let's out a sigh. He knows that he doesn't have a choice. He is penniless, homeless and alone. My poor Dad. He will always have me though. I will never leave his side, ever.

"Do you want a sandwich Dad? Or some chips?"

"Sure son."

I get up and pull my hair back. I position it to wrap it in a bun. I smile because it makes me think of Oliver. He always grabs my bun and says it's a potato. It's the funniest thing ever. I go to swing open the door wall. It's locked. What the hell? Why is the door locked? I peek inside to see Mitch. His back is turned to me. He's dancing. I tap lightly on the glass door. He turns slightly to the left. He is holding a knife.

"Mitch? What are you doing?"

My mind surges to panic mode. Has he lost his mind?

"Dad! Come quick! We gotta break in."

My Dad jumps out of his seat and throws his cigarette into the grass.

"Watch out!"

Episode 5

1

My Dad bangs on the door wall really hard.

"Mitch, can you hear us buddy?"

Mitch turns around looking surprised. He has a knife in one hand and a lime in the other. He turns around and rushes to the door and pulls it open.

"What the heck Mitch?"

"Sorry guys, I didn't see you there."

I sit down at the kitchen table to let my heart rate go back to normal.

"Mitch, why is the music so loud?"

"Ickyduck99 has ten thousand followers baby!"

"Ickyduck99?" My Dad stammers out. "What the hell is that?"

"It's his Twitch name Dad."

"Twitch?"

My poor Dad. He still has a flip phone. Mitch walks up to my Dad and starts dancing with him.

Should I take this opportunity to tell Mitch that my Dad is our new roommate? I'm not sure how he is going to react. Mitch pulls out a bottle of Jack from on top of the fridge.

He is really excited. This isn't a really good mix with my Dad. He isn't the biggest fan of drinking. My Dad opens the door wall.

"Gentlemen, I'm gonna step outside. Congrats to Ickyduck99."

"Thanks Dad!" Mitch shouts.

Mitch pours some Jack into a shaker with ice and closes the lid. He does a few shakes on each side while dancing.

"Baby…." I give Mitch a loving stare. Mitch turns around with a smile. His face drops. He gives me an empathetic look. Being married for so long has given us a gift. It's like we can read each other's minds. Mitch glances outside towards my Dad.

2

"How long?"

"I don't know baby."

"That's okay, as long as he needs to stay it's okay baby. He is such a good guy. Anything he needs, I got his back."

I crack a huge smile. And that is why I love him. Anything I need, he always has my back. Since day one. No matter what I need, he helps me. And he even extends it to my family.

Mitch sets down a shot in front of me and hands me a lime.

"You know I can't baby." I just started an antidepressant. My doctor specifically told me not to drink liquor with it.

Mitch gives me another empathetic look.

"Want me to put a tiny bit with some Pepsi?"

"Okay fine, a little tiny bit."

"We have to celebrate baby, Twitch is going to be huge, I can feel it."

"Can I make an account too? I could play video games."

Mitch busts out laughing.

"Shh, you are gonna wake up Oliver."

"Um baby, if he was going to wake up, it would have happened already."

I guess he's right. I'm always paranoid. I just want him to get enough sleep. Plus, late night, we play hard. As soon as he is asleep, the drinks come out. Blunts get rolled, it's time to get lit.

It's like we lead a double life. I don't mind partying; I just feel more comfortable if Oliver is sleeping.

Mitch sets down my drink with a pink straw and an umbrella. I crack another a huge smile. He really loves me. Mitch kisses the top of my head. He is literally the sweetest man alive.

I take a sip of my drink. Perfect, I can barely taste the Jack. The caffeine mixed with the liquor is such a bad idea. But oh well, I need to party with Mitch. Celebrate. No one is a bigger gamer than him. No one. He has literally been playing forever.

3

It's funny because when we decided to get married, I had no idea he was a gamer and so into technology. I was so poor, living in a studio apartment in downtown. He practically just moved right into my place.

He lived with his large Italian family so he stayed with me so we could have privacy. I will never, ever forget that time. That's when all of the murders happened.

The puzzle piece killer. He literally terrorized the entire population of New York and the neighboring states. I wasn't as scared because I had Mitch to protect me. He never left my side.

We would spend hours in the apartment studying and making love. Such passionate love. Whenever I saw Mitch, we just couldn't get enough of each other. The electricity was undeniable. So, one drunken night, we decided to get married and have children. We didn't care which happened first.

Besides a killer on the loose, everything was perfect. The Puzzle Piece Killer. He would strangle women and leave them in the woods of a nearby park. He had been doing it for months until the first body was discovered. The worst part was what he did to them. He would remove a piece of skin in the shape of a puzzle piece. The part that baffled police and reporters was that each puzzle piece was a different shape.

4

My girlfriend Jolene started coming over every night because she was terrified. She matched his victimology. Mitch was convinced that she was being paranoid. She walked around with Mace spray everywhere. Even to this day she still does.

However, it started a tradition. Once or twice a week, we have drinks and play cards. So at least something good came out of the murders.

"Babe! Babe!" Mitch is waving a hand in front of my face.

"You were zoned out like your Dad does."

"Sorry baby."

"Please tell me you weren't thinking about him again."

I look down into my drink.

"Baby let it go, it's been five years."

The killer gave me nightmares. I became obsessed with the news coverage. Mitch would end up in a rage. He said I was worried for nothing. I would be fine if they would have caught him. But it's like he disappeared.

"That asshole probably skipped the country or killed himself baby, he's gone."

Mitch is right. He's gone. For now. I was convinced that he had some sort of psychological issue. However, I read a study that people with psychiatric illnesses are more likely to be the victim of a crime than the criminal.

Then I was confused. Why on earth would someone do something like that? Mitch, Jolene and I would spend many drunken nights watching the footage on the news and trying to figure out who the killer could be.

"Baby, I can't go through this with you again. We are safe, okay?"

He's right, we are safe.

6

Back to the basement I go. I would rather be on the beach somewhere. I just want to soak up some sun and chill. Moving from California was the biggest mistake ever.

Time to fire up the computer. Noelle is a great guy. He really is. I am not sure about the old man though. Something is off about him. Maybe he has a few screws loose. Hell, who I am to judge? I am not exactly the picture-perfect person.

What do they always say? Ah yes, blame the mother. Should I blame her? For the way that I am? My imperfections. She did punch me square in the face after all. I couldn't believe it. I was only ten minutes late for dinner. I feel like I didn't deserve that.

My nose bled everywhere. Then she whipped me with a cord for getting blood on her nice couch. Who in the hell was she fucking with? I was bigger than her. I could have taken her ass out then. My jaws clench tightly together.

Is this her fault? She is a good mother though. All of the cooking and cleaning. She spent her whole life making things perfect for us. The house always stayed spotless.

6

It was never good enough for my Papi though. He would come home wasted late at night. He would scream and yell at her. She didn't deserve it. She worked really hard. Scrubbed our floors with bleach. Every single meal was home cooked. From scratch.

Women don't do that anymore. It would literally be taboo. Today, food gets delivered. Cleaning companies clean the houses. But Noelle is different. He cooks and cleans. He makes fresh healthy snacks for Oliver. Him and my Mom had their issues at first. But now? They are as thick as thieves.

Noelle learned all of her Italian recipes. They spent hours in the kitchen together. Which was perfect. I needed time to perfect my craft. Creating the perfect puzzle pieces. Guess who's back bitches? What happened? Did you forget about me?

Episode 6

1

Thank God, she's here. I close the text message screen and head to the door. Note to self: delete my text messages. It's not that Mitch would ever go through my phone. But if he did, he might not like what he sees. Ex-boyfriend drama, complaints about his Mom. Oh, and the browsing history of porn. I just can't help it; I don't know what is up with me.

"Jolene!" I hold her tightly in my arms. My best friend in the whole world. The one person always has my back. She knows everything about me. The good, the bad and the ugly. And for some strange reason, she still sticks around. She knows all of my deepest, darkest secrets.

"Hi Noelle!"

Jolene pulls out a bottle of wine. She has a big grin on her face. Perfect teeth. Perfect skin. She is so lucky. She has it all.

We scurry off inside like two teenage girls. We walk in to be met with Mitch. He has a serious look on his face. He looks stressed out.

"Hey baby, are you okay?"

Mitch cracks a fake smile.

"Yeah, I'm fine."

I will have to have a heart to heart with him later. He is so sweet. He might act big and bad on the outside. But inside, he is all sweetness. I swear, I don't deserve him.

"Do you have the cups ready?"

"Of course I do girl!"

Now that the weather is warmer, Jolene and I can get back to our routine. We walk to downtown together. We live in a safe neighborhood but it still feels risky. But fun. Jolene is fun. She is perfect for me. She makes me do things I would never do. Her and I are a perfect duo. A yin and yang. If I didn't know any better, I'd swear we are soul mates.

2

"I need a wine opener Noelle."

I whip open my kitchen drawer and rummage through all of my junk. I pull out my wine opener and hand it to Jolene. She is definitely the dominant one between her and I. Which is hard because Mitch is also very dominant. However, I am very independent. I prefer to do everything myself. It is a power struggle for sure.

I am always trying to keep the peace. So, I let people be themselves. I don't fight it. Maybe it's the Libra in me. Jolene is always bringing up my sign. She is just amazing. So, I let her have her way with me.

Being a stay at home parent doesn't always bring a lot of people into my life. The fact that Jolene shows me so much attention is a shock. And she is so good with Oliver. It's amazing.

Jolene pours the white wine into our pink plastic cups. She snaps on the lids and inserts the straws. Perfect. Just two good looking people going for a late-night stroll. With water of course. We grab our drinks and smile at each other. Let's do this.

Jolene is on bad ass chick. She takes her ponytail holder out of her blonde hair. She is ready to get loose. We head through the living room. Mitch is already settled in on the couch. He already started gaming. This time he isn't live. He is playing just for fun. He is so simple and sweet. He has an innocence about him. It's in his eyes. That was the first thing I noticed about him.

3

"Bye Mitch." Jolene gives Mitch a salute. I blow him a kiss and we walk out of the door. The night air is slightly cool. The smell is so sweet. Spring is so delightful. A time of new beginnings. The snow is gone. People are out and about. Speaking of which.

"Girl, don't look."

Too late, she looks anyway. It's Chance. Honestly, he's a nice guy. Once I spoke to him, he seemed pretty nice.

"Who's that? And why is he sitting in his car with his eyes closed like that?"

"That is our new neighbor. He's nice."

"Oh."

Jolene isn't convinced. She knows that I think everyone is nice.

"He has been having a hard time. He got diagnosed with narcissism and his woman left him shortly after."

4

"I can't blame her."

"Really Jolene?"

Jolene glares at me.

"That's like Mitch leaving me because I have bipolar disorder."

Jolene knows a lot about my mental health but I don't she fully understands. I try to he as open about it as I can, but my struggles are real. The only reason I am stable and doing so well is because of Mitch.

"But you are awesome though."

"Jolene, you came into my life during a good chapter. You have never seen me at my worst."

"Noelle, I know you okay? You are awesome. There is a big difference between you and your new neighbor."

"Okay Jolene."

Let's just change the subject. Some people will never understand. Sometimes, I get so depressed, I don't even know how I can get out of bed. How do you tell someone that though? Like I will open my eyes and I don't know how I am going to make it through the day.

This wine isn't going to help either. My Dad constantly tells me that alcohol is a depressant. He's right too. After drinking, I swear I feel more depressed the next day. Oh well, you only live once right? Might as well have fun.

I have this guilty feeling. The feeling you only get when you do risky things with a best friend. Like if a cop stops us right now, we are completely fucked. You can't just walk around drinking in public here. No one is going to know though. We have been doing this for a few years now. Our track record is really good.

5

"Are we gonna buy some cigarettes?" I give Jolene a big grin.

My dirty little secret number one. Only, Jolene knows about it. When I am extremely stressed out or partying, I smoke a bit. It is absolutely my guilty pleasure. I get so excited about it. Mitch can never find out.

"Of course. We are going to have so much fun!"

This is what life is about right? Letting loose. Having fun. Mitch and I used to have this connection. We were unstoppable. My Mom would take Oliver for a few days and it was just him and I against the world. It was around the time we met Jolene.

We would stay out all night partying. It would end up with one of us throwing up in the morning. It was fun while it lasted. But it came crashing down. I almost put myself in a mental hospital. You can only abuse yourself for so long. Too much drinking and such a huge lack of self-care. I will never forget that day. The day that I realized that my brain had taken too much abuse.

6

Mitch and I were grocery shopping with Oliver. I was talking really fast. My words were making sense to me but Mitch was looking at me like I had five heads. We both looked at each other and we knew. I was headed into mania.

The debilitating part of my bipolar disorder. We grabbed Oliver out of the cart and left our stuff there. Mitch called my doctor and found out that he could see me for an emergency appointment.

We rushed to his office. I could literally feel my brain breaking. Reality was fading. My heart was pumping through my chest. The paranoia was setting in. I could barely contain myself as the nurse did an EKG.

I could feel my body filling up with rage. For no reason, I was ready to freak out. Mitch couldn't save me. I was at the mercy of modern medicine.

Dr. Sansay saved my life that day. I told him in the midst of my crisis that I believed I needed a mood stabilizer. He whipped his pen across a purple prescription pad. It was just in the nick of time. That was a huge wake up call for me. My brain has its limits. Everyone has their breaking point.

As I popped my Xanax and mood stabilizer that day, I was given a second chance. I will be damned if I'm gonna fuck it up.

"What the hell Noelle? What did you do that for?"

Episode 7

1

"Why would you toss your wine like that Noelle?"

"Look Jolene, I can't drink like that anymore. It messes with my health too much."

Jolene looks at me with disbelief. She is convinced that a glass of wine a day keeps the doctor away.

"You are crazy Noelle. Your medicine must not be working."

Really? I can't even speak. What a low blow. I seriously can't even believe her.

"Goodbye Jolene."

I swiftly walk away from her back towards my townhouse.

"You fucking asshole!" Jolene shouts into the dark night air.

Whatever. I don't need her. I can't make her understand. My brain doesn't work like hers. I can't drink like that. I have tried to explain it to her in so many ways. We are supposed to be best friends. I seriously never want to be a best friend ever again. It's too much pressure. If I don't do everything, she says then I am crazy and my meds aren't right. I kick a rock off of the sidewalk into the grass. The anger kicks in. The regret.

2

Why did I let her in? We got so close these past few years. Just for her to get so upset over something so small. Maybe this has been a long time coming.

A red sports car drives by and gives me two honks. Oh yeah? You like what you see? At this point, I'll take what I can get. The street lights light up my path. Well just because Jolene wants to hate on me, it doesn't mean I have to call it a night.

I spot a gas station on the left side of the street. I swear I could just smoke a whole pack of cigarettes. That's dumb though. Why the hell would I abuse my body because someone upset me? That's just stupid. I pull my backpack straps up on my shoulder.

I have a few packages to ship from my store. The post office is only a twenty-minute walk. Jolene and I were supposed to go together. Oh well. I still have a business to run. I need to blow off some steam.

I walk into the Shell gas station. The door lets out a loud ding sound. To buy cigarettes or not to buy them. It seemed fun when I was with Jolene drinking wine. Where the hell did she go? She is known to just run off after drinking. Also, this isn't our first fight.

I walk over to the drink cooler. I grab a bottle of Smart Water. I turn to see a three-tiered basket of fruit. I grab a banana and a red apple. This is more like it. Fuck getting drunk and smoking. I want to live a long, healthy life. Mitch needs me. So does Oliver.

3

I set my fruit and water on the counter. A woman with long strawberry blonde hair smiles at me. She is missing her front left tooth. She has deep wrinkles on her face. Her lipstick is bright red on her chapped lips.

"Hi there honey," she greets me in a raspy voice.

"One second please."

I walk over and grab a Nature Valley bar.

"Okay all set."

The woman starts ringing up my stuff. Her eyes keep darting to a small television set. I can't make out what is on the screen because of the angle. The woman hands me a paper bag. I grab the bag and head out of the gas station.

"Be careful! There are killers out there!" The woman shouts out.

Okay lady. Thank you.

"Goodnight!" I shout back.

This particular gas station is at the top of a hill. A small strip of road lies ahead of me. We refer to it as downtown. The downtown is lined with small, old shops and restaurants. The restaurants seem to stay very busy. But I barely ever see anyone going into the shops. I seriously don't know how they stay open.

Just beyond downtown to the right, is the post office and library. Oliver and I always go to the library together. We hang out in the kid section a lot. But first, Oliver and I go upstairs to the adult section. I grab all kinds of books. I have such a thirst for knowledge. My favorite are the cookbooks. My most recent haul was vegan cookbooks. It seems impossible, but I want to go completely vegan. I am getting a lot of heat from certain family members about it though.

4

My mother-in-law acts like its blasphemy. I remove my backpack, unzip the side and insert my water, apple and bar. I'll keep the banana for now. What does she know anyway? No offense, but she isn't perfect. I'm still undoing the damage she did on Mitch. She decided to treat him like a punching bag his whole life.

I have a lot of respect for my elders. That's the way I was raised. I think she picked up on that right away. She saw it as a ticket to walk all over me. She acted like Oliver was her son. So possessive. No offense, but I don't want Oliver to have the same life as my husband.

Oliver deserves better. That woman is great from a distance. But you can't just let anyone have access to your children. Especially if they are toxic. I know that I have a diagnosed mental illness, but I own it. I get treatment. I take my medicine. My worry is the people who refuse to face their issues.

Or worse, the ones who walk around acting like they are perfect. Okay Noelle, get out of that part of your brain. The negative area. It's over. Mitch's Mother is far away. Life is different now. I pull on the end of the banana and peel three different sections down. I smile as I think of my Dad.

5

He says bananas are his favorite fruit. I always smile and laugh because I know that he will follow that with the fact that they have their own wrapper. I hope it works out with him staying with us. He is a good man. He just doesn't have the best luck with women. As of tonight, neither do I. I love Jolene, I really do. Which is why her and I almost kissed last year.

Her and I were having a blast at an after-hours club. She had just started a new relationship. She was drinking more than normal. I definitely couldn't keep up. She was very handsy and leaned in for a kiss. However, I wasn't trying to take advantage of her.

6

I do like women after all. I remember coming out to Mitch. We had been married for a couple of years. I could no longer deny it. Surprisingly, he took it so well. We agreed that we would basically live a polyamorous lifestyle. It was awkward and scary. Mitch would take me to polyamorous parties and get-togethers.

After trying to live the polyamorous lifestyle, I realized that it was messy and confusing. It fuels a lot of chats between Jolene and I. She is like my human journal. I have had multiple dates and flings with women and Jolene knows all about them.

It is like I lead a double life. It is so confusing sometimes. But being bisexual, that's just the way it is. Mitch is completely cool with it too. I have gone away for a weekend at a time to be with someone before. I couldn't believe he was okay with it.

"Noelle! Noelle!"

"Jolene?"

Jolene isn't one to come and apologize. I never expected her to come running back to me. She is literally sprinting down the sidewalk. Her face is full of terror. I toss my banana and run towards her. Fuck it, all is forgiven. We never stay mad at each other.

"Noelle! He's back!"

Jolene lands in front of me and grabs one of my shoulders. She looks me dead in the eyes. I'm so confused.

"Who Jolene? Who's back?"

Jolene holds up her iPhone to my face. The bright light blinds me.

My eyes widen with fear. Oh my God. That's why the woman at the gas station was concerned. I get it now.

Amy Perez MS Psychology

Episode 8

1

I tried. I tried to hide. I tried so hard to fit in. I gave you guys everything you wanted. I give out smiles. I laugh at all of the jokes. I sip the wine and eat the food. I make the money. But it's all a lie. It's a fat fuckin lie. When you cut me off in the grocery line, I wanna slit your throat. When you almost hit me in traffic, I can see myself pulling you out of the car and beating you to death. I can't hide in the shadows anymore.

The rage has built so high that I finally snapped. This society has built me. The unrealistic expectations. Everyone is fake. It's all a façade. Does anyone really want to wake up at seven in the morning and put on a tie? Fake the whole day? My body is fighting it. My brain cells are screaming. I'm one honking of a horn away from killing them all.

2

Where is this coming from? I was fine. Maybe it's been building for a while. I could just tell Noelle. He could psychoanalyze the whole thing. What would he say? If he knew the real truth about me? The demon. He's possessed. He lives in my head. Sometimes when I look in the mirror, I don't even see a man. It's the Grim Reaper. Ready to turn someone into a ghost.

All of these people living a fucking lie. I see right through it. It's her. Jolene. I can see right through her. She loaded my gun. It's in her laugh. Her smile. She stays hidden behind a face of makeup. Every touch of Noelle's shoulder. Every time she smiles at him. I can see myself plucking her perfect teeth out one by one.

I can feel her moving in slowly. She is pushing me out of the way inch by inch. The jealousy is choking me. The anger is boiling my insides. She won't get away with this. She is using the same tactics I used to put Noelle in my grasp. Her and I are one in the same. We have equal sadistic qualities.

We hide it. We pretend. That's how we survive. But the Jack can't tame me anymore. The weed smoke can't sedate me any longer. I was dead on the inside this whole time. My insides were rotting.

But it was her. She woke me up. I crawled from my grave that society built for me. I'm resurrected bitches. I'm taking her out. This one is just a practice. So were the last ten. All blonde. All perfect teeth. Perfect stand ins for Jolene. These are the practice interviews but

Jolene is gonna give me the job. I plunge the knife deep inside. Sorry honey. Nothing personal.

3

Even doctors practice on cadavers, don't they? It's only fair. Normally I just strangle. But Jolene has made me up my game. I want to make it extra special for her. She deserves nothing less. She has been chipping away at my soul little by little. A tear falls down the cheek of my nameless victim.

"Nothing personal sweetie." I hear screams through the duct tape.

"I have a puzzle to complete."

My practice dummy's eyes bulge out in fear.

"Oh, you know me?"

That's always my favorite part. When I get the recognition I deserve. When my work is finally appreciated. No bonus check could compare to it. I pull a pocket knife from my pocket. A little engraved gift from Mommy dearest.

"Mommy's Angel" is carved into the wooden handle. Is that her apology? Oh, sorry for the multiple bloody noses. Here's a fucking knife. Sorry for all of the unrealistic expectations. Too bad you aren't the doctor I told you to be.

"It's not like she helped me. She shooed me away into my bedroom. She gave me a backhand and a computer."

God forbid I mess up her perfect house. Not a crumb could land on the floor. Not a spec of dirt from the outside could be seen on the floor. For what? For who? What was the point? Who was all of the perfection for? All of the pressure. The abuse. Over a fucking clean house.

4

I swing open the wine opener portion of the pocket knife. Perfect for my artwork. It's special to me. It's what makes me, me. It's an imperfect tool that makes a perfect shape.

"See Mother? I am perfect. Just like you wanted."

I punch my password into my android. I open the Pandora app. I select the classical music station. Perfect. Just what I need to concentrate. Blondie is unconscious now. Also, perfect. I don't want any jagged edges.

Each piece has to fit perfectly together. I was inspired with this idea at ten years old. It was a 3D puzzle of a woman's torso. It was so perfect. I begged my Mother for it. I was in tears. I never asked her for anything. She had all of the finest meats in the cart. Ten bottles of wine. A sixty-dollar cake. Everything had to be perfect for her big birthday party. God forbid I ask her for one fuckin thing.

"You don't need it," she snarled.

"My party is Saturday; how could you be so selfish?"

Where should I make my carving? I don't want any blemishes. No moles or scars. Not one spot. My artwork would be ruined.

5

"Noelle! They found a body!"

"Jolene, I can read!" My body is struck with fear. How could this be?

"They found the body in that park you guys always go to."

"Oh, my Lord."

We have been there a million times. How could this be? I must keep this from Oliver. We have spent so many weekends camping there. So many afternoons on the trails. So many evenings fishing. We practically live there all spring, summer and fall. Mitch knows that place like the back of his...

"Oh my God, Mitch. Jolene, we gotta get back home."

We turn the other way on the sidewalk and start to jog back to the townhouse. This can't be happening. That park goes on for miles. What is it like twenty-mile radius? It's literally a fifteen-minute drive from our place.

The most brutal, heatless killer is here. Right under our noses. How the hell has this happened?

"Jolene, faster!"

Jolene picks up her pace to catch up with me. Mitch is going to die when he finds out. He was so sure that the killer had skipped the country. Or had died. I'm not crazy after all. I fucking told him.

"What a coincidence," Jolene says between heavy gasps. "You get a new neighbor and all of the sudden there is a body."

Leave it to Jolene. That's a little far-fetched. I'll let her believe what she wants though.

"That guy is not a killer."

"How do you know?"

6

"Because I just know."

Jolene and I turn the corner into my neighborhood. I immediately spot my Dad on the porch. There is a cloud of smoke above his head. My car is gone from my parking spot. I land in front of my Dad.

"You millennials exercise at the weirdest hours."

"Dad, where is Mitch?"

"Don't you mean Ickyduck99?"

"Dad, I'm serious!"

"He went to grab some beer and pizza. He wants to celebrate an endorsement he got."

I didn't hear of any endorsements.

"I'm keeping an eye on little Oliver. He is snoring away in his bed."

"Okay, thanks Dad."

Of course. Mitch's late-night hunger as he calls it. He says that he can't control it. One night it's pizza, the next is tacos.

All of the sudden, I feel like smoking. I see the blinds of my new neighbor's window split apart. We are being spied on. An awkward feeling creeps over my body. Why does Jolene have to insert these ideas into my brain? She always seems to be right though.

She was right about Mitch's Mom. She knew right away that she was bad news. I completely missed every red flag. Jolene looks at the parted blinds and then at me. This isn't real. It can't be.

Narcissistic Episode Series

Episode 9

1

"Noelle! Noelle!" Who is that running towards us? Oh. I could never mistake that small stocky build. It's Mitch's brother. Has he lost his mind yelling in the middle of the night? I knew it was a mistake for him to move across the street. He is a great guy though. He is really protective over Oliver. Him and my Dad don't quite see eye to eye. Also, him and Jolene have had their words. Family is family though.

"Gabrielle, be quiet." Jolene says in a loud whisper.

My new neighbor's door swings open. It's Chance. He pokes his head out and just stares at us. Then he slowly closes the door. We all stare at each other. I'm waiting for Gabrielle to tell us a crazy story like he always does. He talks loud and fast. He is covered in sweat. I glance down to see blood on his knuckles.

2

I'm not surprised though. He practices martial arts in his basement. When he was helping us move in, he couldn't get over how awesome our basement was. He said it would be perfect for him to practice his craft.

He literally had a company come in and install wrestling mats, cages, boxing bags and gym equipment. He always comes over all sweaty and gross. And hungry.

He is obsessed with my cooking. Like dude, it is not that great. He always brags about how I learned all of his Mom's recipes. I just learned a lot of cooking styles from his Mom so

Mitch would have another reason to stay with me. Definitely a manipulative move on my part.

Looks like Gabrielle needs food and a shower. His shaved head has beads of sweat all over it. His dark complexion is glistening in my porch light. He storms by us and into the townhouse. He knows I have leftover food in the fridge.

It's kind of like an even trade because he buys clothes and shoes for Oliver. All the time. He will just show up with brand new Nike shoes and clothes from Macy's. I love it. And him.

3

Who does everyone think I am? Some little bitch? Like I'm just gonna back down? I'm not scared of anyone. I'm not a punk. Maybe when I was a boy, I took shit from people. I would let a lot of bullshit slide. But not anymore. I don't know what's been up with me this last few years.

I definitely haven't been myself. It's like I've become a yes man. I've been doing everything that everyone wants. That is not me. I am my own person. I can make my own decisions. I can say No dammit!

It's my time to eat bitches. Ya'll better pass me the plate now. The next mother fucker to even look at me sideways is getting wiped off the map. I can't even blame good old Mother anymore. She's changed. She is a completely different person now.

It's funny how that works. A parent can be a complete asshole and treat you like shit your whole life. Then they wake up one day and decide that they are gonna change. Like really?

You couldn't have done that years ago? Well guess what Mother? The damage is already done.

You already fucked my life up. There is no going back for me. You lit a fire in me. And every smack and harsh word was like pouring gasoline on it. Until I exploded. The sad part is, it took me taking my first life to heal. Her last breath was my first breath of fresh air. How could that be?

4

Thank goodness! Mitch is back. I see the headlights of the Kia turn into the neighborhood. He always makes everything better. His brother is probably being loud in the kitchen so he will have to quiet him down. They are like good versus evil I swear. Gabrielle is the bad boy and Mitch is prince charming. People get into a relationship with Gabe expecting him to be like Mitch but they couldn't be more different.

What I like about Gabe is that he treats his Mom like a queen. He buys her nice jewelry and perfume. He takes her out to eat. He spoils her. Mitch doesn't even call her. I buy all of her gifts. Mitch can be a bit on the selfish side. When his parents come to visit, he won't even give up the bed for them to sleep. He will make them sleep on the couch or a blow-up mattress. We always get in a big fight over it.

Like respect your elders. When someone is older than you, you show them respect. Period. Mitch hops out of the car with a six pack of Guinness. Now that's a beer. Dark and delicious. I don't know if it is because I am Irish, but as soon as I tasted Guinness, I was hooked. So smooth and perfect.

Mitch leans into the car and pulls out a pizza. It's Jolene's fault. She got us hooked on beer and pizza. I had never considered pairing the two until I met her. She changed my world for sure. She is definitely my girl crush. Or my idol, I'm not quite sure yet.

"Hey guys, what's up?"

We are all just staring at Mitch. He doesn't know. He's clueless.

"Is everyone okay?"

"He's back Mitch."

5

Mitch looks puzzled. He turns and sets the pizza on the car followed by the six pack. He takes out a beer and pops open the top.

"I know, I am back."

Jolene's eyes get wide.

My Dad blows out a cloud of smoke.

"Yep, and I am his side kick. We are the puzzle killers."

Jolene's eyes fill with rage. I'm used to my Dad and Mitch but she's not.

"You two are assholes." Jolene sets a cup on my cement stairs.

"Goodnight."

Jolene storms down the street towards her car. I know better than to chase her. When she's pissed she stays that way. It will be up to her when she calms down.

6

Blue and red lights light up the street on the road leading to our house. Two cop cars turn fast into our neighborhood. They both pull up and block in my car. What the hell? My Dad looks at Mitch. Mitch looks at my Dad.

"Damn, we were just kidding man." My Dad puts out his cigarette on the porch.

Nobody moves. No one says a word. This could be bad in so many ways. Knowing Mitch, he probably just picked up a dime bag or more from a buddy.

Gabe sometimes dabbles with cocaine. And my Dad sort of has a checkered past. This is totally not good. The cops stay in their cars. One is staring at us and the other is pecking away at a laptop. My Dad has taught me to act very proper in front of cops. Yes sir, no sir. All of it. Mitch's parents must have skipped giving him and his brothers that lesson. They seem to think that they are invincible.

7

They have a major chip on their shoulder. I don't want to think it's an Italian thing. I try not to generalize or stereotype based on a few examples. Are these cops going to come out or what? The suspense is killing me. And I'm scared to death.

I have a few hundred dollars to bail Mitch out if he's caught with weed. It's only legal medically. I wonder how much trouble he is in. Dammit. We were just getting ahead. He is going to get fired. I can't afford all of this on my own. I can feel my face getting hot. The air feels cold on my cheeks.

All of the sudden, the front door swings open. It's Gabe. He's wearing a white tank top. He has a plate of spaghetti and meatballs in his hand.

A spotlight hits him on the chest. A skinny white cop jumps out of his car and draws a gun.

"Nobody move."

Gabe's eyes get wide. Please don't fuck up. This can't be real. How do I explain this to Oliver? He doesn't deserve this. What did you do Gabe? What the hell did you do? You guys better not move, someone is going to get shot.

Narcissistic Episode Series

Episode 10

1

Am I laughing inside or crying? Am I screaming or dying? That was a close call with the cops last night. Reckless driving? Some old white asshole is just gonna tell the cops that I was driving fast behind him? And they just take his word for it? And come fuck with me? That is some white privilege shit right there.

They could have blown everything. I felt untouchable until last night. It's so fucked up. You can do everything right. And some asshole comes out of nowhere and tries to fuck your life up. They could have searched my house. My basement.

My masterpiece would have been ruined. I only need fifty more puzzle pieces. But when I am done, I don't care what they do to me. Haul me off wherever the fuck you want. I just want Mother to see. That's it. Then I can die a happy man. Like she ever gave two shits about me. It wasn't until I got older that she saw the benefits of being in my life.

She acts like I can't see it. Like I am some dumb ass fool. When will my intelligence be celebrated? I am smart, hardworking and valuable. Is it a female thing? Do they all just look down on men? Like we are worthless?

2

It's all fun and games until you wanna get married and have a baby huh? Then we have value. Like really bitch? A man's company isn't enough? Our companionship? Why are we the ones paying for strippers and prostitutes? We buy you for time and attention. Both are free. All you have to do is sit and listen. Maybe laugh and smile. That's it. Why is it so hard?

Everyone will learn though. There is a price for their behavior. I fire up the computer. Time to do some research on my young ladies. I have it down to a science. I might have to do some traveling.

With the discovery of the recent body, security is gonna be tight at the park. It was fun while it lasted. My days in the sun. The trees. The wind. It was perfect. Another example of some asshole taking something perfect from me. Why is society like that? Anything good just gets taken away. Why can't a man be left alone to practice his craft?

Let's see what my computer has to say to me. I take a sip of my Starbucks. Ah. Breathe life into me. I'm desperate. I peel open my banana. I dig into the sweet flesh. Fuck! All of my stocks are tanking. Why? If only I jumped in on Facebook, I would be chillin' right now. I'd be sitting on my own private island somewhere.

But no. I'm stuck here with the commoners. Calling the cops on me for driving. What the fuck. Oh Earl. You should catch my wrath. But you won't. You will sit on your nice comfy couch reading a book. Like I'm just some nobody piece of crap. Just like everyone else. That's fine. You do you. I'm gonna do me.

Maybe I should sell some of my stocks. Technology is sucking right now. Noelle was saying something about marijuana stocks. He is smart. I will have to look into this. I need to make some cash. I won't miss this one. Everyone and their Momma seems to love smoking weed.

3

You lazy bastards. You need help sitting on your asses? Really? Well so be it. Give the people what they want. Let's see here. Let's do my picks. I got a few thousand to play with, why not. ERBB, MDCN and MJMJ. This better pay off big. Take my money dammit. I'm not missing this train. Early bird gets the worm. You gotta hit the market when it opens. You can't just wait until noon when you finally roll out of bed.

Now let's head over to social media. I'm not looking for cat pics and dumb ass videos though. I'm after one thing. Her. Jolene. My next project. She can have any guy she wants. She could easily take her pick. She has every trait that men are looking for. Hell, even women can't deny her beauty.

She would put these Instagram models to shame. She doesn't see it though. She doesn't see herself the way I do. Shit! I'm a little too excited now. I will have to show her exactly how I feel. Oh Jolene. You don't know what you do to me. This is the moment when most guys would send a dick pic huh? Good thing I'm not most men.

I will show her my obsession in better ways. How was karaoke Jolene? I see you look very smiley. How is the new boyfriend? He looks innocent. Let's see, some videos on helpless animals. Jolene, you almost make it difficult. You are a really good person, really. But you stepped on my toes. You took things too far.

4

"They found more bodies!"

Mitch looks at me dumbfounded. Doesn't he care?

"Babe! He is back!"

"I know that! What the hell do you want me to do about it?"

Oh, I don't know, care. Give a damn. Show some emotion. Someone is knocking at the door. I jog over to look out of the peep hole. It's Chance. He really is a nice guy. I swing open the door.

"Hi Chance!"

"Hey, how are you? Is there any way I could use your hose? My outside water isn't working."

"Oh sure, no problem. Come on in."

"That was crazy how those cops showed up."

"Oh yeah, people can't drive fast anymore huh?"

"I guess not." Chance looks around nervously. We head out of the back door. I walk down the steps towards my hose. I untangle the mess. I haven't used my hose yet this spring. Usually I am feeling more ambitious when the weather breaks. What did my doctor say? Oh yeah. Seasonal affective disorder. The winter time actually makes me suffer from depression. It makes me want to pack up and move somewhere tropical. But I can't. My entire family is here. I would rather deal with weather depression. I don't want to be sad and miss them. They are my rock and I am theirs.

5

• • •

"Are they going to catch this guy?" Chance is hovering over me.

"Oh, I hope so."

"Me too."

"I have a child to raise, I don't really feel confident with a serial killer out there." I whip the hose from the side of the townhouse.

"I know right man. What kind of society are we living in nowadays?"

Mitch steps out onto the back porch. Coffee in hand. He is so cute and sweet. I just love him so much. He definitely needs a haircut and a nice shave. He always puts himself last.

"Hey Mitch, you doing some gaming today?"

"Nope, I'm heading into the office."

"That's great," Chance flashes a big grin. "You don't wanna put all of your eggs in one basket."

Mitch is being patient. Chance is being a bit of a jerk.

"Gaming isn't exactly gonna put food on the table."

Mitch shoots me a look. I shrug at him. I can't control this guy. What am I supposed to say? I actually put food on the table from having an online business. So, what the hell does this guy know? I hand him the hose.

"Thanks Noelle. It's nice to know that good hearted people still exist."

"No problem."

"Oh, can you do me a favor?"

"Sure Chance, anything."

"Can you tell your Dad to stay off of my grass?"

What the hell? Has this guy lost his mind? I should grab my hose back. I really can't help what Mitch says at this point. I wouldn't try him. He is super nice. But his boiling point is much lower than mine.

6

I turn to make sure that Mitch isn't ready to throw a punch. But to my surprise, he isn't there. I'm suddenly feeling alone and vulnerable. Did he purposely wait until Mitch walked away to say that? Now if I say something, I'm going to look crazy. This is so not cool.

Jolene was right. She's always right. There is something up with Chance. That is not normal. I can look beyond a lot of things. But that wasn't cool. I know my Dad isn't perfect. But I told Chance that he is going through a break up. I poured my heart out to him the other night.

This is my repayment? I thought we had an understanding. My brain isn't feeling normal at the moment. I run inside to talk to Mitch. He's gone. I reach for my cell to call Jolene. Straight to voicemail. That is definitely not normal. Did I just fall into the twilight zone?

Amy Perez MS Psychology

Episode 11

1

Instagram time. Time to study. The behavior of the divine species. Women. Let's see what the live videos have to offer. A makeup tutorial. Not exactly thrilling for me. However, it helps me gain information. I can't even get a woman to say hi to me. But she will divulge everything on a live video to a bunch of strangers. It makes no sense.

And what is it with makeup nowadays? Women are spending hundreds if not thousands of dollars to look like wild animals. Haven't people heard of natural beauty? Have you ever thought to ask a real man what he likes? I'll tell you what, we don't like to be fooled. Just be yourself. I bet this woman will do her makeup and look like a totally different person.

It's completely unfair. When I was a boy, Mom would put on some lipstick and blush and go out to get groceries. Those were the good days. When women actually cooked. God forbid we ask for a home cooked meal. How many followers does this woman have? Let's take a peek shall we.

Fourteen thousand? What in the actual fuck? Why is makeup that interesting? Sure people. Let's spend our days educating ourselves about the newest makeup trend. Whatever you do, don't pick up a fucking cookbook. When did women get so entitled anyway?

2

You needed a man in order to be created. Did you forget that? Men serve a purpose you know. I just can't stand it any longer. You need us for survival. Not that women care anymore.

It's actually cool to not have kids. Go figure. My Mother should be a part of my generation. She should have skipped having kids. Do everyone a favor. She never gave two shits about me. It was obvious that I was a burden.

Sorry raising me was so difficult Mother. It's not like I fucking asked to be here. Would it have been so hard to at least give me the time of day? Pretend that you care? Maybe take me out for some ice cream or pizza? I'm so sorry that I ruined your life. I really am. Thank goodness for social media though. It does help me see that there are some good moms out there.

3

I can't even believe it. Some of these women have an entire page dedicated to their children. Sure, being a Mom isn't perfect. But they damn sure make it look beautiful. Where would I be if I had a Mother like that? One that made me the star of her life? One that didn't bitch and complain about my existence?

These women give me hope. Happiness. In a world full of hate. There they are. The people that will nurture the future society members. Because what are we without love? Acceptance? Care? What happens when we don't get hugs and smiles? We are cold. Heartless. We are dead inside. We feel unworthy. Unwanted.

When someone pushes you aside because their wants are more important than your needs, it hurts. Like Hell. The pain cuts deeper than any knife. And no one can help you. No one can save you. It's a deep internal wound. You will forever feel like no one cares. You will doubt any love that you ever find.

Which is why I do what I do. I cleanse society. From people like this makeup hoe. Sure, worry about your face while your children do without. How much food so you have in the cupboard huh? When's the last time you sat with your children? Gave them a piece of you. You think those thousands of followers give a fuck about you?

No honey. They don't. But I do. I care a whole lot. I just picked up a new research project. You. It doesn't mean that you will be part of my masterpiece. But you make a good candidate. I have to study you first. Follow you. But it isn't me. Oh no. I am just another woman like you. You see, on the internet, we can be anyone we want. Even a dead girl. Thanks to my last victim. All I had to screen shot her photos and crop them.

4

"Oh my God Jolene! Thank you for finally answering."

"Are you okay Noelle?"

Jolene is always such a concerned friend. She feels like more than a friend. Not quite like family though. The love is definitely there.

"Yes, my love, I am fine. I just had a super weird moment with Chance. Now it's raining so I am feeling down and tired."

"Why don't you go lay down Noelle?"

"I would, but I have a ton of studying to do."

"You better get started!"

"Let me call you back later."

And that's what friends do. They make you feel better. They draw you out of the darkness. I used to underestimate the power of friendship. I didn't always see the point. Also, I was never even a good friend. I don't even feel like I am a good friend to Jolene. I seriously don't deserve her. If she were to straight up walk out of my life, I wouldn't even be surprised.

Let's see, I have three exams this week. How am I supposed to pass them? I know that I am smart, but I have to prove it. Human growth and development will be easy. Research and design will be a bitch for sure. I hate stats. Maybe I should drive over to the study hall. I just want to crawl in bed. Not that I want to die or anything, living is just so hard.

I just feel so low and depressed. I can't shake it. As soon as it's morning, I dread the whole day. I don't enjoy things the way I used to. I'll have like small moments of happiness but they are occurring less and less. It's like the lights of a building shutting off one by one.

It's like all of the doors slamming in my face. I can't stop it or control it. It's not just in my brain. It's my body too. I just feel sluggish. Like I just want to stay in my bed or lie on the couch. Why can't I be normal?

I need to take a shower too. My hair is greasy and my skin feels itchy. I just can't bring myself to do it. I feel like the shower beads are going to feel like pins and needles on my skin. Is that anxiety talking? I swear, I can't even pinpoint which disorder is talking.

I should just give up, shouldn't I? Throw in the towel. I mean, what's the point? I look around my disheveled environment. Blankets on the floor. Dust everywhere. Dishes in the sink. I'm worthless. I can't even manage my own space.

5

Why am I like this? My brain starts to feel haunted. I start remembering every negative thing anyone has ever said to me. All of the hate people portray onto me. It doesn't help when you are already feeling low. How do I drag myself up from here? From this place? Is there someone I can call? What can I do? I feel like I am mentally drowning mixed with panic. I wish there was a magic pill to make these feelings go away. Who or what can save me?

Gabriele. Gabe can help me. He is always there when I need him. Conveniently, he is right across the street. I slip on my Nike sandals and head out of the door. I run across the road between our row of townhouses.

I bang on Gabe's door. Come on I need you! I can hear loud music from inside. Maybe the door isn't locked. He says he isn't afraid of anyone and he barely locks his door. I twist the knob. It's open.

"Throw dirt on me, grow a wild flower." Lil' Wayne blares from the basement. My favorite song. I'm already feeling better. I run through the living room then the kitchen. I stop at the basement stairs. Am I being intrusive? Maybe I am crossing the line. The basement door is closed.

6

"Gabriele?"

I hear some faint moaning sounds. Oh. That's a woman. I am way out of line. What on earth am I doing? Who just busts into a single bachelor's house like that? I am definitely invading privacy.

I turn to leave but something catches my eye. There is a mannequin in the kitchen. It looks like the one I use to sell clothing online. Why would Gabe have one? I walk closer to examine the mannequin. I seriously cannot believe my eyes. There are faint lines drawn in pencil. There are over a hundred puzzle piece outlines carefully drawn out. Panic and fear shoot through my body.

I am paralyzed. It feels like my body just turned to cement. Gabe? Gabe? This has to be a prank. He must be fucking around. I carefully step back through the living room and leave though the front door. To my surprise I see Jolene's car. She must have been worried about me. I jog back to my place. My Dad confronts me with my dog. Boots is pulling my Dad at full force.

"I am determined to train this boy!" My Dad exclaims as he is walking towards us.

"Dad did you see Jolene?"

"No son, I just walked out for a smoke."

I run inside to grab my phone. Where the fuck is Jolene?

Episode 12

1

It's a curse. Bipolar Disorder. It's me versus Gabe. Will my stigma outweigh what I just saw? Who do I tell? Who can I call? I need to call Mitch. How in the hell do I tell him that his brother is a killer? I mean that's pretty crazy. My brain doesn't feel right. If I'm not careful, I could end up in a psych ward. I love Mitch but how did I end up in this mess? His whole family. It's like a curse. My head is spinning. I can feel the impending doom setting in. My heart is pounding.

Quick Noelle. Ground yourself. Look at your surroundings. Notice your feet on the ground. Pictures. Look at the pictures of your son. Everything is okay. I take some deep breaths. Okay. I'm calm to an extent. Thank goodness for my awesome therapist. She helps me through all of my issues. I could call her. Would she lock me up? Dammit. If I was normal, I wouldn't hesitate. Did I imagine what I saw?

Am I hallucinating? Surely Gabe is not the puzzle piece killer. There is no way in hell. Maybe that is just a practice dummy. Maybe it represents the puzzle piece killer. That would make sense. My heart rate slowly goes down to a normal pace.

2

Okay. But I still need to see my therapist. Jolene. Her car was right outside. Did I imagine it? I am so confused. My medicine has been working so well. It can't be me. I dial Mitch's number. I hear his ring tone in the house. What? I thought he was at work. This can't be right. I run up my carpeted stairs to look for him.

"Mitch?"

The ringing grows distant. Okay he isn't up here. Maybe he's in the basement. I swear he left.

"Mitch?"

I call out for him. Nothing. I whip open the basement door. Nothing. The ringing stops. I hit his number in my cell again. I'm losing it. I'm losing my mind, aren't I? I hear the ringing. His phone, it's in the basement. I can hear it. I go as fast as I can down the wooden steps. I see Mitch's phone on the desk next to his computer. No Mitch.

That's strange. He isn't one to leave his phone. I hear some creaking in the floor upstairs. These townhouses are about twenty years old. Then I spot it in the middle of the floor. It's Coach. Jolene's purse. It's definitely hers. Brown, cross body Coach purse.

3

"Jolene?"

My brain is swirling. Grounding is out of the question. I'm freaking out. No, I'm dying. My chest and brain are going to explode. My normal is gone. No, it's shattered. Who the hell do I call? Mitch and Jolene are out. Gabe is questionable at the moment. If I call the cops,

they will probably take me to a mental hospital.

Oliver, oh my God, Oliver. Thankfully he

is at school. I glare at my phone. He gets out in

three hours. I can calm myself by then. I can't

take a Xanax. If I do, I will need to sleep it off.

Weed makes more sense. It helps me. But it isn't

legal. Fuck it. A couple of puffs won't hurt. It'll

calm me down.

I know just where Mitch keeps the joints.

He is really good at rolling joints and blunts. I

open his desk drawer and sure enough, there

they are. I grab a tightly rolled joint with a

shaking hand, spark it up and inhale slowly. Yes.

That is all I needed. My lungs fill up with the weed smoke. Calmness takes over my body. Just a couple of hits and I'll be good to go. I take a seat at the computer. I pull the ash tray closer to me. I can feel a calm washing over my body. My brain has reached an equilibrium. I take another small hit off my joint. That should be enough.

I don't want to get too high. Messenger. I can reach Mitch through Facebook messenger while he's at work. I turn on Mitch's computer. I never touch his stuff. He always tells me that I can. But I like him to have stuff that's just his. He doesn't understand it. But I think it helps someone have individuality. Also, confidence.

Just imagine having to share absolutely everything just because you are married. That would be crazy.

4

We all need certain stuff that's just ours. I click on the Facebook icon. Mitch's account pops up. I get the urge to be nosey. I always look through his stuff but I never find anything. I always feel like an asshole for snooping through his stuff. Like what in the hell is wrong with me? Mitch is a really good guy. He honestly probably deserves better. His Mother seems to think so. She is constantly finding things wrong

with people. Like bitch, you ain't perfect
yourself. Stop it Noelle, that's not helping.

Why is Jolene's purse in my basement?
Do I go look for her or message Mitch? Let me
try to reach out to Mitch. I still have an urge to
snoop through his messages. I usually just snoop
through his phone. The computer is uncharted
territory. Fuck it. I'll just tell him I was trying to
figure out where he was. I click on his
messenger inbox. Just some boring stuff with his
coworkers. Nothing new. Last time I did this, I
saw some messages from a woman. She was
using heart emoji's and I got super pissed.

Jolene and I were at a diner and I told her about it.

We convinced each other that Mitch was cheating. After three cups of coffee and some greasy food, I was ready to confront him. I busted through our front door super crazy that night. He was just innocently playing video games on the Xbox. Poor Mitch, he doesn't even like women. Unlike me. Wait, who the fuck is this bitch? She looks like a damn stripper. Mitch hasn't read it. But I will. And it's getting deleted.

5

Hey Ickyduck99, I love your live feed. I am a rep for Starbucks and I was wondering if you would like to do some advertising for us.

Well don't I feel like an idiot. I am paranoid. It's probably because I have feelings for Jolene. It's so wrong. I guess I feel like if I can fall for her, he could fall for someone too. I hate my brain sometimes. Why does my brain work the way it does? My mouth is a little dry. I grab an iced coffee out of Mitch's drink fridge. He was so against it when I ordered it for him. What did he call it? Oh yeah, ghetto fabulous. Whatever though. While you are high as fuck playing video games it's great isn't it? I don't see him complaining now.

I open the cap and take a sip from the glass bottle. That would be sweet if Mitch could be a rep for them. What does that mean? Hopefully we can get free coffee. It'll help with my early mornings with Oliver and my late nights studying. Shit. My classes. I seriously need to study. I am never going to graduate.

I still feel like snooping. The feeling is itching at me. Why? I log out of Mitch's Facebook. I trust him. I really do. Everyone does. He is the picture-perfect guy. I take a sip of my sweet and creamy drink. I love this stuff. I could drink it all day. What the hell do I say to Mitch? Hey baby, I love you. By the way, your brother is a serial killer.

"Hello? Noelle?"

6

It's my Dad.

"One second!"

I love my Dad. Just the sound of his voice feels like home. I'm glad he is staying with us. I just want him to be good. I should take him to get some food with me and Oliver. I feel like a plate of food right about now. Let's send Mitch a message and see what's going on.

I open up the Chrome browser. The images shock me. I cannot believe my eyes. Dead women. Pictures of dead women splashed across the screen.

All of their lifeless eyes are staring at me? How? Why? How can this be happening? This isn't real. This can't be reality. Mitch, message Mitch. But I'm stuck. I'm paralyzed. The images are burned into the back of my retina.

The perfect puzzle pieces dug out of their skin. The pictures are so detailed. I feel a chill all the way to my bones. Message Mitch, call my therapist. Find Jolene. I can do this.

.

Episode 13

My whole life, I've been waiting to die. Like when is it going to happen? Will I get by a car? Shot? Stabbed? Will I be ready? Will I show up in Heaven? Burn in Hell? Maybe that's why I am so fascinated with the process. Like what is the point of life? Honestly. I just keep up the façade. The fake smiles. But my smile today is real. I have her. Ms. Jolene. Don't worry honey, this won't last too long.

I never know if I should practice my craft before or after death. Typically, it just depends on my emotional attachment. It's funny how that works. I could feel more emotional attachment to someone I just meet than my own family. My own Mother. Except for Mitch. Mitch knows everything about me. Everything. He planted the seed about Jolene.

I couldn't imagine it. But now that I am here, the feeling is amazing. Which is why I am waiting for him to get here. He has to see this with his own eyes. We both hate this bitch. She ruined our lives. She corrupted Noelle. We were better off without her.

Like who does she think she is? She is such a feminist. The fear in her eyes is priceless. Surprise!

2

She didn't think I was listening. But I overheard her giving Noelle an earful about me. Well guess what? Now it's time for me to show you how I feel about you. That's the funny thing about feelings. They are never one sided. Take every feeling you have for someone. They also have a feeling back.

But it's hard to tell which feeling is true with all of these fake ass people, who knows? Everyone wants to judge you. They will take something so trivial like your looks and use it against you. Like really? My fucking looks? A tooth out of place or a gray hair. Really?

Fucking fake ass trolls man.

Some bitch will go to a fucking salon and come out looking down on people. Even though she looked like a dead animal an hour before. Contemptuous bitches. Jolene is a perfect example. She represents all of the women that are too good for guys like me.

I mean I match energy. If you ride for me, I ride for you. Period. Too bad my Mom didn't understand that. She could be chillin' right now.

"Look what you've done!

"Fuck!"

Oh well. I can't change it. I need to get the fuck out of here. My space feels disheveled, unorganized. I'm gonna go blow off some steam at the gym. I need a clear head for this one. Plus, I am not sure of the level of involvement Mitch wants.

Does he even see the reality? He seems to idolize me. He says that I do the things that he only dreams of. That is the problem with people today. They just dream. Like if you want something, bust your ass to get it. It's that easy. Look at me. I have my own place, money, women. Everything. What else could you really ask for?

I have the life that everyone dreams of. Sorry Jolene, I gotta go. I lean down and kiss Jolene's wet forehead. It's okay sweetie, this will be epic.

3

"Hello? Um yes, I was calling to have someone check on my brother-in-law."

What in the hell was I thinking? Why would I let having bipolar disorder stop me from going for help? If something isn't right, you call. Period.

"Yes, I heard some screaming and fighting from inside the house."

Do I think something is really going on? I'm not sure at this point.

"Thank you, officer."

Now we wait. I'm sure Gabe is going to be super pissed. But what can I really do? You really have to trust your gut. It will show you the way. I feel such a mixture of feelings. Guilt. Nausea. Righteousness. I'm tired of being so paranoid dammit. Yes, I have a mental illness, so do many, many other people on the planet.

I have to be sure dammit. That is my bestie. If she is in his house then this is all worth it. I know I heard a woman in there. And her car is here. Sorry Gabe, but Jolene comes way before you. I love her. I am in love with her. Now, it's time to prove it. She has shown me her love time and time again. I was just too blind to see it. Fuck it, I'm not waiting for the police, she needs me!

4

I jog, then sprint across the road. Up the cement stairs. I bust through the red door and through his house. Music blasting, no other noises. I go to open the basement door. Shit. It's locked. Shit. I need a knife. I run through the kitchen and grab a butcher knife. I jam it in between the door and the door frame. Thank god

I have experience breaking in houses. I sprint down the wooden stairs. I can't believe my eyes. It's her. Jolene. She is wearing a black bra and panties. She looks pale. She has a rope tied into her mouth.

"Jolene! Jolene!"

Jolene turns to me. A look of relief washes over her face. I hold the butcher knife up to the rope and slide it back and forth. Dammit! It's thick. Fuck! Jolene is squirming in the chair.

"Dammit Jolene! Stop moving!"

The rope disintegrates in my hands. Next for her wrists. Gabe is fucked. I am gonna fuck his ass up! It's over asshole! Hands untied.

Jolene jumps up and wraps her hands around my

neck. She is crying into my shoulder and

squeezing the life out of me. I love you Jolene.

Jolene leans back and stares into my eyes.

A big smile crosses her face. She is beautiful.

Without warning, she kisses me so passionately.

Her lips feel like heaven. It's more than I could

ever dream of. I reach down and feel the lace of

her black panties. She is a dream. She smells

delicious. I grab her hips and kiss her with

everything I have. We go straight to heaven.

This is exactly what fate feels like.

5

This was meant to be. I lean back and stare into Jolene's eyes. A huge smile crosses her face. She is so perfect.

"Noelle, I have always loved you. Thank you for saving me."

I have so many words for her. I don't even know where to start. The only way to tell her would be to show her. Let my body do the talking. But not here. Not now. We need to get the fuck out of here. Jolene grabs between my legs.

Oh Jolene. Apparently, she has other plans. I unclip her bra. She's amazing. Super model status. I lower my head and kiss the soft

skin on her neck.

Jolene unzips my pants. Her hands are

shaking. I lift Jolene against the stairway. Wrong

place, wrong time. But I can't help it. My body

is screaming for her. Jolene moans softly into

me ear.

"Noelle, I wanted this since the moment I

saw you."

Jolene takes me further into heaven. She is

so damn amazing. Take me Jolene. Please! How

did I get so lucky? I am the luckiest man alive.

The need for her is so strong. I can't stop. I

won't stop. Ever. Jolene grabs my neck and gives it a sexy squeeze. She is such a bad girl. I can't believe it.

"Jolene, I love you."

Jolene holds a finger to my lips. She pulls me deeper inside. Then our connection is complete. We stop and stare at each other. She is an angel. We softly kiss and feel each other's bodies. Where are we going to go from here? Where does this take us? My mind has been lit on fire.

"Baby, let's get dressed."

By the look in her eyes, she wants more. We need to get out of here though. There will be plenty more of this though. Jolene grabs my face and shows me that she really wants me. Wow, she is such a freak. I can't right now. But I feel the need to. This must have been brewing for quite some time. All of the laughs and smiles. Our connection. It led to this.

Why didn't I see it? She has always wanted this. I've been so fucking blind. I am going to marry her. I need to be with her. She is my forever.

"Jolene."

She doesn't let me speak though. She kisses me once more. I slide my hands up and down her soft body. I can't resist her. She is so intoxicating. I'm in love.

What is that? I hear footsteps upstairs.

"Jolene!"

But she doesn't stop.

"Dammit Jolene!"

I pull her away from me.

"Someone is here!"

Jolene pulls up her panties. I pick up her lace bra from the floor. Footsteps hit the stairs. Shit. It was worth it though. It was so worth it.

"Neither one of you fucking move!"

Episode 14

1

There is no cure for this. No treatment.

But what if there was? Would I take it? I feel

like I'm the normal one. These new dudes are

fuckin' soft. They don't make them like me

anymore. Lucie would know. All she had to do

was love me. That's all I asked for. Oh yeah and

a little fucking loyalty.

Some guy would come along and show

her a little attention and that was it. She would

be head over with some guy trying to get in her

pants. Like really? All of the cards, the flowers,

the dates, the sex. I gave everything to her. Everything.

So, when I saw the messages in her phone, I had no choice. The rage lit a fire in every muscle I have. She had to die.

She had to pay for fucking me over like that. I wanted her to feel my pain a thousand times over. But she couldn't. Because she was dead, that was it. Her life was gone. She didn't even feel empathy for what she did. Like men were just toys for her to play with. Why Lucie? Why? You Slut!

That's all you will ever be. That's it. But you are gone. You can't be jealous. You can't send me any angry texts. There is no makeup sex. I need you Lucie. Give me a sign. Where do I go from here? You have your way of guiding me.

2

"Mr. Meseret" it's time for your meds."

Of course, just when it was getting good. Why must they interrupt me? I set my pen on the notepad. Oh well, there is that blonde chic out there. She is bad. But like a good bad. Let's see

where she is. I'm getting better now. That
depression had me on my knees man.

My baby momma was trippin' too. Thank
God she dropped me off here. I don't know what
she is always worried about man. She ain't gotta
go to the salon man. She is gorgeous inside and
out. I was attracted to her natural beauty. She
was beautiful from the start. There is no need to
spend hours at the salon. All I wanted was her. I
wanted to hear her laugh. See her smile. Her
voice is like heaven. Lucie and I are supposed to
be together. Why do I do the things that I do?
When she found those Instagram messages, I
knew it was over. Why? Why did I entertain

those women? They are all just so fake. Why
was I so damn stupid? Man let me get the fuck
up out of here.

"Mason! Come on man! Come get your
meds!"

Ah, look at what we have here. Little
Bonnie finally fell asleep. Her man looks like
Scarface though. I've never seen someone so
manic before. Some people in here are lifers.
They ain't never getting out of here. That is the
worst. She'll recover though. She's got her man.
Some people in here ain't got no one. Their
whole family done walked away.

I got my family bringing me brand new shoes and basketballs and everything. Man, that time I saw fire had me fucked up. I guess I'll just take my pills and chill. That suicide shit had me fucked up though too. It ain't nothing to play with.

I am here on this planet for a reason. I can feel it now. Maybe I can get a job as a Psychologist. That would be epic. I am pretty empathetic. I have a gift. People always tell me that I make them feel good about themselves. I am a good guy. Never mind all of the assholes that teased me for being too smart or too short. God forbid all of the racist people. They don't know any better. That's for God to judge, not me. My intentions are good so that's all that matters.

"Fuck you too asshole!"

"Ma'am, you need to calm down."

Oh shit, they are gonna have to take her ass down again. Thank God she's in here. I can't imagine her running the streets like that. She would end up in jail or dead for sure.

"Look snowflake, you gotta take your pills."

Oh good, the mental health tech. Thank God she actually listens to him.

"Amy, your Dad is on the phone."

And just like that, her Dad brings her down to earth. Every time. That man is like God or something man. Look at her calm her ass down. Hopefully they know she hallucinated the whole basketball thing. I literally passed it lightly to her.

Please God, help us. It's definitely not our fault that we are like this. Everyone that helps us are angels sent from above.

"Here you go Mr. Meseret."

"Thank you, Ma'am."

"You're welcome sir."

Narcissistic Episode Series

Schizophrenic Episode Series

(Preview)

Narcissistic Episode Series

Amy Perez MS Psychology

Narcissistic Episode Series

Episode 1

1

"Excuse me sir! Are you okay?"

Who is that talking? I look up in the night sky. They are coming for me. I know it.

"Sir, is that your car smashed down the road?" I gotta run! I throw my cigarette into the grass and take off into the field. They will never get me. My chest is pounding. My body is aching. Blood is dripping from my forehead and elbows. I gotta get outta here man. I gotta find my brother. He can get me out of this mess. He was always good at fleeing the scene.

"Sir, stand down."

No way man! I grip my cigarettes in my front pocket. "Sir! You are surrounded!" Oh yeah? Watch this asshole!

I turn around to see six blurred figures surrounding me. Too bad they are no match for me. I grew up in the south boys. I can wrestle anyone in the grass. Three of you are too overweight to even catch me. I might not be the strongest, but I'm quick. As lightning.

First comes a left hook. Contact. Yep they don't stand a chance. Next a right kick to chubby's cheek. Take that asshole. You think you can really mess with me? Two short men approach me. One has a black shiny stick in his hand. I grab their necks and throw their heads together. They crumple to the ground. Goodnight boys!

This has got to be a joke. A tall skinny guy with red hair approaches me. He is wearing a blue shirt and slacks. You think you can take me huh? Take your chance young man. My knees are bent. My fists are out right in front of my face. Whoever he is, he is about to meet his friends on the ground. They can't mess with me! I'm King David!

2

Come on slim! Show me whatcha got. I don't have all night now. If these aliens show up, I'll be the least of your problems. God has sent them. It's the only way. Why do you think I'm here? I'm going to save us all. I have to. For my girls. Carrie and Dana need to have a good life. These alien cocksuckers are not getting to my family. Just wait until I get to their headquarters.

A skinny left arm swings by my face as I dodge it. I let out a wild laugh. I should just let the kid go. The other guys were cocky. They deserved it. But him? He's just a kid. A child. He reminds me of me. I used to be a little guy. I was skinny with red hair and freckles. I was a shrimp in comparison to my older brother. He was gigantic. Which is why I need to find him. I'm locked eye to eye with the kid.

Maybe we can meet at an agreement here. We can reason with each other. He's young. He might be easily manipulated. Not that he needs to be. These huge aliens are going to wipe us all out. There is a secret agency that has been protecting us but they are failing. Aliens are coming from everywhere.

"Come on kid, just let me go, and we can both walk away from this," I beg. I don't want to hurt him. I hear some groaning from the ground. It's chubby. I kick him in his stomach. Stay down.

"Sir, I can't do that." He reaches for something in his belt. A knife? A gun?

"You don't understand slim. They are coming for us. Any minute now there is going to be aliens everywhere."

The kid lets out a loud laugh. Really? You think it's funny? It won't be funny when they suck the eyeballs out of your head.

3

I fake a punch at his face with my left hand and swing my right leg back and boom! Round house kick to the temple. Whoops. Sorry kid. I really didn't want to. His skinny body crumples to the ground. I check his belt. What was he reaching for? There is nothing there. Hhmm. Weird. I see something shining in the grass. I walk over and peer at the object. Shit. It's a gun.

I'm not trying to take any lives here. The last time I shot a gun was when I was sixteen. I was in the backwoods of Tennessee. My Pa taught my brother and I how to shoot a shot gun. Even though my brother was ten years older than me, I could always keep up. If Anthony shot a peasant, I would shoot two. I could always one up him. Sometimes he would let it slide and sometimes he would get mad and competitive. Sometimes we would end up in the grass to fight it out.

"Goddammit boys! Knock that shit out!" My Pa would shout at us. He tried his best but the alcohol would take over him. It turned him into a monster. You couldn't even recognize him. You wouldn't wanna piss him off. He took it all out on my Ma though. I lost count of how many times I visited her in the hospital. Bruises and cuts would cover her body.

I pick up the small handgun from the grass. I put it into my back pocket. This could come in handy. I don't want to use it but if I have to I will. I might need to pistol whip chubby if he tries to get up. I reach for my front pocket. Phew. My cigarettes are still there. My menthols. My lifesaver. As long as we have the cigarettes, we are good to go. I just wish I had an ice-cold pop to go with my smoke. I grip my cigarette pack and stare down at the six bodies lying around me. Nice try boys. No one is going to stop me. I must protect my little girls. Two Teethers and Pumpkin.

4

I take out the soft pack of cigarettes from the pocket of my blue shirt. Almost a full pack. I pull out a one hundred. I take the Bic lighter in my hand and light up my cigarette. My mouth fills with smoke. I don't inhale though. I never inhale. Only an idiot would do that. Why would you fill your lungs up with all of those chemicals? I'm not stupid.

I studied at the seminary after high school. I was the top of my class. I was teaching the pastors all about the bible. I had read the bible over one hundred times. There was nothing they couldn't teach me. I may not always preach the bible to everyone but I act like a believer. I kick some gravel as I walk down the road. I ash my cigarette into the grass. I take another hit. The menthol fills my mouth. I gotta get to Anthony. We can be a team.

Anthony is the only person I can trust with this mission. It will be him and I against the aliens. I saw the master alien before I crashed my damn car. I just bought that car too. Elizabeth was pissed. She didn't understand why I came home with a brand-new car. She didn't understand. How do you explain to your wife and kids that our world is going to end? There was no time for words. I remember my wife screaming as I was getting into the car. I was trying to bring our dog as my copilot. But she was screaming at the top of her lungs.

I know I was angry but she didn't understand. There was no time to explain. I told her that Elliot and I had a mission. It wasn't a lie. But Elliot the sheep dog wasn't coming home. I was tired of him shitting all over my house. And the scratching. He would scratch all day and night without stop. I just couldn't take any more of that damn dog. Until I found his purpose. He was going to have a front row seat to the end of the world. With me.

5

I take a drag off of my cigarette and fill my mouth full of smoke. There is a chill in the air. It's fall in the North. It's right around Carrie's birthday. My little Pumpkin. She's only seven years old. She has golden blonde hair. She's an angel. Dana is growing so fast. They need their Dad to be a hero. Elizabeth doesn't get it. This problem is bigger than us.

She doesn't understand me. I work ninety hours a week to put food on the table. All she cares about are her damn animals. She could try and care more about me than a bunch of animals. Ten pets are too much. I can feel my forehead wrinkled in anger. I needed to get out of there. I couldn't take it anymore. I was just going to clear my head. Until I saw him.

God. He came to me. He spoke to me of the invasion. It was a message for me. I was on a back road in my small town. Next thing I know I'm here. Where here is, I have no idea. I need to find a street sign or something. It's so dark out. Maybe I should walk back and find my car. Those men should be gone by now. They really didn't see that coming did they? A smile crosses my face. I'm pretty quick.

My brother is in Georgia so if I could just get there and explain everything to him, we will be good to go. I got enough cash in my pocket to get there. I can take a bus. But first I better stock up on smokes. I take a long drag off my cigarette. God, I could use a little guidance right about now. Whatcha got? 1992 is turning out to

be an interesting year so far. Ow! Dammit!
What was that? I see red as my body hits the dirt
road.

6

It's chubby. My hands are handcuffed
behind me as I struggle to get out. He was a cop.
They were all cops. This isn't good. Not at all. I
need to call Elizabeth. Chubby gives me a nasty
look. He has a big black eye and a bloody lip.
"Yes, we are processing him right here. Do you
want us to hold him here or bring him tonight?"
A young woman with black hair is on the phone.
She stares at me with a concerned look on her
face.

I look down at my front pocket. Dammit.
My cigarettes. Their gone. I need my smokes. A
Coca Cola would be nice too. My mouth is filled
with a dry feeling. My head is pounding. How

did I get here? My eyes feel like they are wide open. Like I couldn't close them if I tried. My muscles are filled with adrenaline. The chubby cop just stands there staring at me. Who's the big man now is what he's probably thinking. Yeah, he is pretty sour over the fact that I took him and his buddies out.

They came up to me. They interrupted my mission. Don't mess with a man on a mission. As soon as we clear this up, I can get back to my business. Who do these people think they are? You can't just sneak up on a young man in the middle of the night like that. They made me drop my cigarette. "Okay, thank you." The dark-haired woman hangs up the phone.

"Mr. Clark, we are going to hold you here overnight in isolation and tomorrow you will be transferred to the Columbia Correctional Institution."

I stare at her blankly. Chubby is munching on a cheeseburger as his mouth parts open in a smirk. Then he busts out laughing exposing a mouthful of chewed food. I've had enough of this asshole. The cop comes closer to me. I jump up and head-butt him in the chin as hard as I can.

7

He falls like a ton of bricks to the floor. That'll teach him. I'm immediately rushed to the ground. It was worth it. That guy had it comin'.

"Mr. Clark! Stay down sir. Do not attempt to move." A voice is yelling in my ear. All I see is red. My vision goes blurry.

"Andrew can you hear me? I am with the Wisconsin State Police. Do not attempt to move." I feel a piece of steel pressed against the back of my head.

They don't understand. This problem is bigger than us. We are slowly getting invaded. The aliens are not going to back down. I need to get to my brother Anthony. Tonight. I feel cold metal clank around my ankles. There are two men with their knees pressed against my back. I can't see a way out of this one. Shit. A need a sign God. What do I do now? I'm lifted up by three men and dragged down a hallway filled with cells. The beige paint is being chipped away from the metal bars. The floor is covered in a dusty film.

The men drag my body into a cell. My head bangs into a metal toilet. I can smell a strong scent of urine. The metal doors slam behind me. My feet and hands are completely locked up. I can't move. My face is pressed against the damp dirty floor. My breathing is labored. There is a pounding in my chest. My blood is pumping so hard that it feels like my veins are going to burst. My eyes are burning.

My cell door whips open. In a flash I feel kicks all over my body. Black boots stomp the floor after each wail. I'm wincing in pain. I feel each bone getting hit. More like crushed. Dammit. Shit. I'm dying tonight. What have I done? I'm so sorry Two Teethers and Pumpkin. Daddy tried to save the world. I did everything I could. Daddy loves you.

8

I look up to see a barred window. Small slivers of sun shines through. Parts of my body are numb. Others feel so achy that I can't move. I lick my lips to taste that familiar iron flavor.

Blood. There is a pool of blood and saliva on the dirty floor below my face. I can hear men talking and laughing in the distance. My wrists and ankles are still shackled together. My mouth feels like a desert. All I can smell is urine. I hear thick boots hitting the floor towards my cell.

"You put Mikey in the hospital you know Mr. Clark." My mouth is too dry to speak. That bastard is probably happy. Free vacation. He'll lay around for a month and collect a disability payment. He'll be fine. He deserves worse for how he was antagonizing me. That man knew what he was doing. He tried to piss me off on purpose. More importantly, I need a cigarette. Like now.

"You're getting transferred in a bit Mr. Clark. Don't you worry. We're gonna put you over with the big guys."

The big guys huh? Are they bigger than you? Because I'm not too worried then.

"Oh, and we spoke to your wife, she is too far to make it right now to bail you out."

Elizabeth isn't going to understand any of this. What in the hell were we fighting about anyways? She really is a good wife. And the mother of my children. Why does she make me so angry sometimes? How did I end up in Wisconsin? They are our neighboring state. I was trying to go south over to Georgia. After the image God sent me everything is such a blur. This urine smell is so toxic. I wriggle my body to lay in a different direction.

Three men approach my cell. "Mr. Clark." We're here to take you to the big house."

The cell door whips open. The men grab both of my arms while my body is dragged into a plastic chair. Chains are attached to each ankle as the previous cuffs are removed. The officers stand me up.

"Come with us." I limp along with the officers. I definitely have a broken bone or two.

9

They are cleaning out the cell. I can smell the bleach. It reminds me of the time with my victims. All of the body parts are still fresh in my mind. The sex. My power. I can still feel the power I had over them. Yeah because you drugged them. Shut up! Shut up! You don't know anything. They wanted it. They just didn't know it. They wanted to be dominated by me.

I paid them the fifty bucks. If only I could go back and finish my alter. I would have ten skulls. I could be reclining back right now staring at my work. It took years to obtain all of those bones. And the taste. I just can't get the flavor out of my head. The human flesh. The muscle. The skin. I loved fileting the muscle from the bone. The process. There is a hardening between my legs. Every day I relive them and it's torturous. I want to be back out there.

Apartment 214 was where they were. Night after night of fun. I miss the alcohol. I wish I had a shot and a beer right about now. I miss the alcohol. But I miss the sex and the flesh more. If I could just have one more of them. One more taste. The muscles were tough but I could perfect the preparation process. I just needed more time. My time was cut short by the one that got away. My big mistake. If it wasn't for the last boy, I would have my alter of skulls right now. I already had nine.

"Right this way Mr. Clark. Your cell is ready for you."

Ah who is this? Fresh meat? He's handsome. Mr. Clark huh? He has thick brown hair and a nice build.

"Can I get a cigarette please?"

"I'll see what I can do Andrew."

Nice name too. Andrew. I like it. He has nice blue eyes to go with it. He is much more handsome than any of the other men. I would love to eat his heart out. "Time for a shower Gavin." My cell swings open just in time to get one last look. Hi Andrew.

Narcissistic Episode Series

Episode 2

1

I finally got my thirty minutes a day. If only I could get some alcohol. I'll have to settle for a shower. It's hard being locked away for twenty-three hours. My mind is going crazy.

"Ten minutes Gavin." The guard is direct and assertive. He reminds me of my Father. Where is he now? I need him now more than ever. He didn't care about me before. Shit! The water comes out so cold. I don't have enough time. I need to mull some things over. I need the water to scald my skin. I deserve to burn for what I've done. Although I'm sorry, I can't take away the urges. I feel like the devil. The devil himself spawned me. I can't get the taste of the flesh out of my mind it's intoxicating.

"Five minutes sir." Goddammit! I need more time than this. Electricity surges through my veins. I just want to fry myself in this water. I want it to be over. I want these impulses to end. What's wrong with me? "Water off Gavin." I didn't even get enough warmth. I need to feel alive. The only thing that makes me feel alive is the flesh. The blood. I dry off my thin body. I won't last in here.

Many of the men are large in here. I could never subdue them. Not without drugs. I am weak in here. I don't have my weapons.

"Right this way Mr. Clark." Mr. Clark again. Why is he here? He doesn't fit the cliché of the men in here. He's different. It was in his face, his demeanor. I peak my head from the shower. I see a large silhouette of a man being led through the showers. His ankles are chained.

He must have done something serious. Could he be as bad as me? Worse? Dammit. I need a drink. I'll take a nice shot and a cold beer.

"Sir would you like to make any calls or play basketball?"

The guard is big and thick. His light skin is met with freckles and red hair. Basketball? Is there alcohol out there? I'm dying for a drink. I yearn for a taste of blood as well. I could subdue the guard outside. He's not my type though. But a kill could get rid of the voices. Even for a moment. They keep haunting me. There is a monster inside me. I have to let him out.

"No, I'll go back to my cell."

2

"Would you like some shampoo Mr. Clark?"

Shampoo? No. I don't want shampoo. I want to go home. I want my kids.

"No thank you." Why am I here? I'm not supposed to be here. Who can get me out of this? If I don't complete my mission, we are all screwed. I rub the soap on my body. I can't remember when I last showered. The water offers some clarity as the blood washes off my body. God? Can you come to me? I need some answers. What do I do next? I won't abandon the mission. I will complete it at all costs. Even if I have to get through all of these people. My little girls need me. They need their Daddy to do what's right. I just want to see their smiles again. My Pumpkin and Two Teethers.

I have to accept that I may never see them again. I knew when I accepted this mission that it was a one-way ticket. Elizabeth wouldn't understand. She didn't grow up the way I did. She had the perfect life. Her parents live on a lake. They gave her a life that I could never dream of. All of the parties. All of the endless celebrations. She never saw her Mom get beat to a pulp. She never saw a drunk man stumble in every night. She doesn't understand what we went through. My siblings and I never had a home. We moved around so much. We were always at the mercy of the next landlord.

Why can't she see what I'm trying to do? I want my little girls to have a good life. I want them to have everything I didn't. Even if it costs me my life. I would do anything for those little girls. I want them to see. What do they think I work ninety hours a week for? My job. I need to speak to them. I need to explain. If I don't complete this mission, my job won't be there anymore. I have until Devil's Night. The aliens have given us an ultimatum. Bring them The Word of God or this world is going to burn.

I'm going to give them The Word of God alright. I know first-hand how mighty he is. God came to me when I was only five. After falling off the back of our porch he came to me. He gave me three months in a coma to show me. They only had to drill three holes in my head. I remember it like it was yesterday. My Ma stayed in the garden for hours. She picked tomaters and green beans. I can practically smell her cooking. She was so busy, she missed me falling off of the porch.

3

I would do anything for a slice of her cornbread. Skillet style. She made that cornbread so thick and rich.

"Five minutes Mr. Clark."

Wow. This the longest shower I've had in a while. I was always in a rush. Those two little girls keep me so busy. I can barely use the bathroom and brush my teeth, much less shower. They are the reason for everything. What's next God? Tell me what to do? Do I stay here? Do I flee? What's the next part of the mission? If I don't get to the meeting slot before Halloween, our world is doomed. I need to get ahold of my brother. He needs to know. We are being punished for our actions.

What did we think someone would think of us? All of our sinning, our greed. Aliens from other planets have been watching us. They are not happy. But I can prove them wrong. I just need The Word of God. Will they want to see a bible? Will my word be enough?

"Water off Andrew, dry off and get out. You can play some basketball or make a phone call."

The walls of this shower are caked with dirt and mold. I'll be lucky not to catch an infection in here. My years as a custodian have taught me enough to know that these conditions could be deadly. Does anyone clean this place? I grab the towel from the hook. It's tainted brown. I dry off my hair and try to wrap it around my waist. It's too small. This is humiliating.

I open the small green curtain when I see it. His eyes. Their red. Supernatural. They've infiltrated the facility. The aliens. His hair is red and his eyes are too. And he has gills. He is not human. God has shown up. I must take him down and escape. I am quick. He's a big man but I can take him. As soon as he turns around, I will strike. He must have some super powers though. I have to do this though. For my girls.

Here's my chance. I can see the veins in the side of his neck pulsing. He's not human. No one has eyes that red color. These aliens are satanic. The Word of God may not even get through to them. I could choke him out. Or strike him in the back of the head. Then I can make a run for it. All of the sudden I feel metal shackles clasp to my ankles. The red eyed alien reaches back and hand cuffs me.

4

Too late. If I take out big red, I could lose valuable information. I need to find out all I can from these people. What do they want? Will the word of God reach them?

"Do you want to go out in the yard or make a phone call?"

I should call Elizabeth. She won't understand though. I don't want a lecture. I don't want to hear her get upset with me. She will understand at the end. It's better to ask for forgiveness than permission on this one.

"I'll step outside," I reply to the guards. "I could go for a smoke if ya got one." Silence. Fat chance of getting a cigarette in this joint. I have been reduced to an animal. Or a possession. They have taken over my body but they won't take my mind.

No one will ever take my mind.

"Sir we are going to put you in a cell around the corner to change." The guards lead my naked body to a cell. It's dark and dingy. My skin is still moist from the shower. The guard takes off my cuffs. The red eyes. Where is he from? Why is he here? Has he come for me? He won't stop my mission. I don't care who or what he is.

"Do you read the bible?" I ask him. There is a long pause.

"I'll get you a cigarette and some clothes," he sighs. Have I reached a common ground with him?

Have they heard of the good book? Do they know of Jesus? I feel cold, moist and shriveled up. The cold bars offer little comfort. My wet feet swipe across the dirty floor. Feces stains the metal toilet in the cell. There is a brown stained mattress. My body surges with disgust. This is torture. Big Red returns with a stack of clothing, pair of sandals and a perfect looking cigarette. There really is a God. He has just shown me a sign.

I can get through to them. If I can show them the word then they will know that us humans are good. Maybe I am in this place for a reason. My next step is to get a bible. I need to show them. I need to teach them. I might be coming home girls. This mission was interrupted for a reason. This fortress is the new meeting place. Everything happens for a reason. I set my cigarette on the stained mattress. I slip on the orange pants on over my damp legs. I slip on the plastic sandals. I slide the orange shirt over my head. There is a perfect sized square pocket on the left side of the shirt. A perfect place for my smoke. I slide the cigarette into my pocket.

5

I'm ready to go outside. I need a taste of freedom. Big Red comes to my cell. A short dark-haired man walks up behind him. He has the shackles in his hands.

"Can we trust you to just shackle your legs?" The short man asks. His white teeth glimmer through his dark skin. He trusts me. Is he one of them? Are they from the same planet? We are going to have a meeting here aren't we? But they have to make sure that they can trust me. I didn't exactly make a good impression when they abducted me did I? It's not my fault. They attacked me. These people caught me off guard.

"I'll behave," I lie. No promises. If I get a sign that I need to do something drastic, I will. The world is depending on me.

They need me in a big way. The short man opens the cell and walks over and shackle my ankles. They lead me out of the shower area and through old metal doors. The rust is taking over the edges. The plastic sandals are uncomfortable between my toes. My feet slide while they are cuffed together. This is my new normal. Like an animal I am led to the outdoors. A small red door leads to the outside.

The ground is damp. There is a small yard with an old basketball court. The net is hanging down. Yellow, red and orange trees surround a metal fence. Barbed wire is curved high to keep us in. Or is it to keep people out? I step out into the wet grass. I breath in the damp, cold fall air. It's almost Pumpkin's birthday I am here for a reason. I have to make sure she has many more birthdays. I hope she understands. Daddy had to.

I reach into my shirt pocket. I grab the long cigarette. This is Elizabeth's fault. I never smoked before I met her. She kept pressuring me. She didn't want to smoke by herself at her parent's lake house. I would do anything for her, doesn't she see that? But six cats and a dog are too much. I can't take it anymore. I didn't grow up that way. I had a dog once. Spot, a small beagle. My Pa took one look at him and took him for a walk. Spot never came back. Anthony and I both heard the gunshot in the distance. My Pa didn't have patience for a dog. Or any animal.

6

It is kind of ironic that now I am basically an animal, the way they drag me around this place. I have no rights. No freedom. My metal shackles drag between my legs as I check out the yard.

"Yo Andrew!" The short guard yells from the doors. He has a big white smile with gapped teeth. And something beautiful and yellow in his hand. A lighter. I start walking towards him as fast as my shackles let me. He meets me half way. "Man, what are you doing in here Andrew?" He lights the lighter towards my cigarette. I put it to my lips and breath in the flame. The end of my cigarette lights in a ball of fire as the tobacco shrivels up. I inhale the smoke deep into my lungs.

I never inhale but I need the high from the nicotine in here.

"You don't want to know," I tell him. I don't want him to fear me. I need him to hear the word. The word of God can heal all of us. I should know, I've read the bible countless times.

"What's your name boss?" I exhale the cigarette smoke away from his face.

"James sir, my name's James. I'm up here from Alabama." I take another puff off of my smoke.

"You're a long way from home ain't ya?" He's lying. My ass he's from Alabama. He made it up on the fly. I'm not leaving this yard, am I? I probably have until I finish this cigarette and my time is up. I know too much.

James smiles and walks back towards the door. He stands in front of the door with his arms crossed. He looks up at the sky. Where are they at boss? They're coming, aren't they? I take one more puff of my smoke. The smoke fills up my lungs. I never inhale. This is a special occasion though. I exhale the smoke and toss my lit cigarette in the grass.

"What do you want from me?" I yell into the sky. "Come and get me you assholes!" I throw my hands up in the air. "Do what you want to me!" Just don't take me girls. I'll give you what you want. I don't need a bible. The Word is all in my brain.

"Hey Andrew man, you aight over there?" James shouts out to me.

Do I look alright to you boss? I feel drops of water on my face. It's time. I bend down and then fall into the wet grass. Just do it already. Beam me up. I close my eyes tight. This is going to hurt. The rain drops fall on my face. This is for you girls. I'm doing it all for you. I hear footsteps trampling through the grass. I open my eyes to see Big Red and James. A needle stabs into my left thigh. A dizziness takes over my brain and I fade away.

7

"Just put him back in his cell man." Who is that getting dragged down the hall?

"What are they doing out there?" The guards seem upset.

"I don't know man; he was yelling at the sky and then he fell in the grass. He was hysterical."

Hi Andrew. His lifeless body is dragging by my cell. If only I could get ahold of the drugs they have in here. I would like to sedate somebody like that. Andrew's head drags on the floor as they drag him by his shackled feet. I'm feeling quite turned on by this situation. If only we had a joint cell. This night could be more fun than normal. Oh hello Mr. Andrew. We will be meeting soon. I practically feel a knife stabbing through his muscle.

I can feel the blood trickle down my arm. So warm. Andrew we are going to be the best of friends. I want to learn everything about you. Where are you from? How did you get here? The cold metal doors to his cell slam shut. The police took everything from me. I almost had enough human skulls to make a full alter. What was I thinking letting that last guy get away? He stopped the monster. But the monster is inside of me. He will never go away. It's because you are a sinner! Shut up! Shut the fuck up! You don't know me! I have to let the monster out. I need blood. I need flesh.

"Gavin, your dinner is here." A young pretty woman yells from down the hall.

"Thank you, Monica." If I liked women, she would be my pick. Her long dark hair covers her breasts just so. She has perfect lips and long legs. She is thick in all the right places. If I looked like her, I would be more accepted. She walks up with a big smile.

"I see you got a shower today." Barely. I wouldn't call that cold water shit a shower.

"How are you feeling today?"

How am I feeling? How the fuck do you think I'm feeling? I'm an animal. A monster.

"I'm good, ya got any beer?"

Monica lets out a big laugh. She is so easy. She's easy to talk to. She smiles easy. And her laugh. It's infectious.

Her perfume hits my nose from outside my cell.

"I wish," she replies through her laughter. "You sure are charming Gavin." She unlocks a tiny door that is large enough to slip my tray through. Ugh. Meatloaf. It's the worst meal in this place. It's not like my Grandma's. At least I had her. My parents may not have been around but at least she seemed to accept me. Even though she didn't approve of me with the men, she still let it happen.

"Thank you, Monica." Her soft skin looks like a dream compared to my littered brain. I wish I could trade places with her. The men would flock to me. Society would accept me. I wouldn't have to hide anymore.

8

I set the tray down on my bed. The green beans are watery. The mashed potatoes look like clay. The roll is hard as a rock. I'm forgotten about. I'm being left here to rot. You deserve it for what you've done! Shut up! Shut the fuck up! I can't keep the monster inside forever. "Aaahh!" I swing my tray around sending the disgusting food flying all over my cell. The meatloaf smashes against the wall. Mashed potatoes hit the ceiling. "Shut the fuck up! I can't take it anymore!"

I bash my tray against the metal cell bars. Over and over. Get out of my head! Damn you! Monica comes running down the hall. She takes one look at me and runs back the other way. Shit. The one person that was nice to me. Now she knows. I can't hide anymore. Footsteps come pounding down the hall. A group of men armed with nightsticks line the front of my cell. "I'm going to let him out!" I scream at the top of my lungs. "He's coming out!" The guards have helmets on and shields in front of them. They can't stop the monster. No matter how hard they try, he won't go away. Nobody can stop this.

"Gavin, we don't want to hurt you," the big man with red hair yells out.

Really? It sure looks like you are trying to do just that.

"Just lay face down on the mattress with your hands behind your back."

Okay fine. Do your magic. Give me the shots. Take me to the psychiatrist again. I don't care anymore. I want him gone. Make him get out of my head. "Please make him stop." I lay down on the mattress face down. I've done this enough times to know the drill.

Pieces of green beans squish against my face. I'm vile. I'm hopeless. I just want it to stop.

The cell door unlocks and slides open. The men enter my room one by one. The handcuffs slap tightly on my wrists. I'm lifted up by force. My arms stretch back behind me.

"We're going to medical again Gavin."

Yeah, no shit. It's the only way. I'm getting what I deserve. The guards stand me up. Mashed potatoes squish between my toes. I can't do this anymore. I can't keep him inside.

9

"Let's go sir." I'm led down the dark and dingy hall towards medical. This is the walk of shame. Monica stares at me with fright in her eyes. We were just joking about a beer. What happened? The rage. I can't control it. I can't keep it in anymore. My brain is exploding with urges. Who is this? A man's body is lifeless on the floor in his cell. His clothing is soaked, grass is everywhere. We walk by his head. It's Andrew. Oh Andrew. You will learn.

We are not allowed to act out in here. Not even a little bit. We are treated like animals but we can't turn into one. The moment we let out the real us, they cannot handle it. I can handle it Andrew. You can show your true self to me. I will understand.

"Stop staring and start moving sir." The guards yank on my arms. Why not just put a collar on my neck and pull me with a leash? Next comes the pills. The voices. The hallucinations. These people don't know me. They don't know what they are doing.

I walk the walk of shame to medical. They think they can just drug the monster inside me. But they can't. I've tried. Countless nights of drinking never took it away. I can't be tamed. I need blood and flesh. No pill or injection will ever change it. Please just destroy me. I can't take it anymore. The compulsion. The rage. The monster. He knows me. He tells me what to do. If I feed him, he goes away. I pay him with flesh. Once my alter of skulls was complete, he was going to go away. It was promised.

No one will ever understand. The torture. The control.

"Pick up the pace Gavin. You gotta see the doctor."

I move my bare feet faster. The food is still caked in between my toes. There is dirt sticking to the food. Andrew will understand. I saw it in his eyes. He's genuine. There aren't many people like him. We will meet somehow. I just have to clean up my act. I need one person to understand. I want someone to meet the monster within. The only people that met the monster are dead. They gave their life to subdue him.

Made in the USA
Monee, IL
18 June 2020